About the Author

Throughout his career in teaching and education consultancy, Paul has developed a fascination with the amazing life stories of those who have gone before us. Women and men facing ever changing social norms and life's challenges, within the timeframe of where and when they lived. His passions include genealogy and travel, resulting in his books being based in places visited and fondly remembered. Actively engaged in community affairs, being Rotary District Governor and chair of his state's Duke of Edinburgh scheme, he has had the opportunity to interact and learn from a range of people.

The Sail Maker's Legacy

Paul Erickson

───────────────────────────────

The Sail Maker's Legacy

Vanguard Press

VANGUARD PAPERBACK

© Copyright 2024
Paul Erickson

The right of Paul Erickson to be identified as author of
this work has been asserted by him in accordance with the
Copyright, Designs and Patents Act 1988.

All Rights Reserved

No reproduction, copy or transmission of this publication
may be made without written permission.
No paragraph of this publication may be reproduced,
copied or transmitted save with the written permission of the
publisher, or in accordance with the provisions
of the Copyright Act 1956 (as amended).

Any person who commits any unauthorised act in relation to
this publication may be liable to criminal
prosecution and civil claims for damages.

A CIP catalogue record for this title is
available from the British Library.

ISBN 978 1 83794 129 2

This is a work of fiction. Names, characters, businesses, places, events and
incidents are either the product of the author's imagination or used in a
fictitious manner. Any resemblance to actual persons, living or dead, or actual
events is purely coincidental.

Vanguard Press is an imprint of
Pegasus Elliot Mackenzie Publishers Ltd.
www.pegasuspublishers.com

First Published in 2024

Vanguard Press
Sheraton House Castle Park
Cambridge England

Printed & Bound in Great Britain

Dedicated to those who left their family and homeland in search of a better life. To Harold (who called himself the old timer) who took the time to listen, remember, research and retell his family's amazing and unique stories, the accounts of facts, secrets, exaggerations and some pure fiction, which constituted their lives. The final betrayal, a memory that would only fade with time and passing generations.

Chapter 1

Lizzie stood at the front gate, staring down the street, hoping for someone, but expecting no one. She had taken time to curl her hair and was wearing the black brocade dress that she normally kept for best. She realised she was fiddling with her pearls, something she did when she was anxious or nervous.

Across the road, Mrs Martin was being her usual self, her lounge room curtain slightly askew a sign that she was watching. Lizzie didn't care. Though she had become reliant on her for help, what Mrs Martin thought was irrelevant. Regardless, to prove she hadn't gone mad, Lizzie checked the mailbox before turning and walking back up the painted concrete path.

As she approached the door she called out, 'Charlie, those bloody dogs are staring at me again,' but as usual there was no answer. She kept walking through the doorway, determined that this time she would throw the two porcelain dogs in the dustbin. She had planned on doing it on many occasions, but each time, at the last minute would feel guilty; after all, they had belonged to her husband's parents, and her son had always implied that one day he wanted them. The two dogs sat facing outwards, reminding her of the emptiness that confronted her. She could not remember a time when she felt so completely alone and isolated.

Lizzie had always prided herself on being in charge. She considered it her strength and her independence, but her sisters thought her to be bossy, and often vain, and behind her back, called her "The Lady". She knew her husband spoilt her and where possible pampered her, but didn't she deserve it?

She picked up the two dogs but rather than throwing them in the bin, she carefully hid them out of sight in the back of the china cabinet. Perhaps now they were gone, she might have a change in fortune. The last few years had been hard; she had lost so much and dreaded what might lay ahead.

There was a knock on the front door but she chose to ignore it. What if it was one of those telegrams? The thought made her body shiver, she couldn't take that. Calming herself she realised it would only be the busybody from across the road or the priest hoping to hear her confession or get a donation for his latest appeal. She didn't want to see either. All they did was bring up the past, and though she thought about nothing else, they were her memories and none of their business.

Distancing herself from her relatives had been her choice. They annoyed her, so she stopped answering the phone and where possible avoided leaving her home. It was here that Mrs Martin had proved useful. She seemed unexpectedly eager to do shopping and messages and had also offered to act as her power of attorney as everyone else had left her, or at least that's how Lizzie felt.

No longer being prone to tears, she sat steely faced, a prolonged and intense, mirthless look, not at anything in particular just at the emptiness that surrounded her. Her expensively decorated formal lounge room, once so important to her, now only acted as a repository of past treasures. She closed her eyes, trying to recall happier times.

Chapter 2

Elizabeth O'Sullivan had been the fourth child of two Irish emigrants, Joannem O'Sullivan, born 1845 in Castlemaine, Ireland and Bridget Delia Corrigan, born 1853 in Fermanagh, Northern Ireland.

Elizabeth's mother, Bridget, had arrived at Port Phillip, Melbourne on the *Colonial Empire* in September 1872. This was a three mast, wooden hulled clipper owned by Aberdeen White Star Line that had left Plymouth, England on the 24th of June and arrived at Port Phillip on the 24th of September. The journey to the colony of Victoria in Australia had taken ninety-three days, the ship carrying 437 passengers. Of these 191 were Irish with 115 of them single girls like herself. Bridget, aged twenty, had travelled in steerage, the lowest deck and below the water line, but as an unassisted migrant. Her father had given her enough money to fund her voyage as he wanted his daughter to have options; accepting assisted passage would bond her to an employer who she may not like or in a place that was not acceptable. The ship's records listed her profession as farm housekeeper. She had boarded the ship carrying all her worldly possessions in one large carpet bag. When she had met her fellow passengers many were like her, with pale skin and freckles, reddish hair, and in her case pale blue eyes. As it was summer most were in similar woollen skirts and blouse top with a shawl over their shoulders. Bridget carried her heavy woollen hooded cloak, thinking it could also be used as a bed covering for extra warmth. On her feet were her sturdy brogues, low heeled boots with decorative perforations.

Bridget had found the ship's matron, a Miss Walford, to be pleasant enough but very strict about routines and assigned cleaning during the voyage. Travelling steerage, most of the journey had been cooped up below decks but on fine afternoons they were allowed on the main deck for exercise. She was pleased that the single female passengers had their own designated section of the ship, separated from families and single males. She contented herself with writing her journal, describing daily routines and recording some of the stories told by the other girls about why they had left home and what they hoped to find in the colonies.

At the time, clippers like the *Colonial Empire* were the pinnacle of sailing ship technology. The streamline hull and acres of sail meant they were built for speed. With the prevailing westerlies on the Great Circle sailing route, passage was fast if not comfortable. Bridget was expecting cramped conditions but was appalled by the squalor. In bad weather she was confined without ventilation or light, the use of candles limited and often forbidden. The straw mattresses were infested with flees and mites and once wet began to rot. Several of the girls became sick and though the matron tried to keep them isolated, the risk of contamination was every present.

Bridget's father, Paugeen Neddy Corrigan was a stone mason and as Ireland had faced severe economic downturns and a series of famines, he supported Bridget's decision to go to Australia in search of better prospects. He had lived through the 1840s and seen the death and disease that came from hunger. Between 1841 and 1851, Fermanagh had lost 41,000 or twenty-five percent of its population with towns like Clanawley, Magheraboy and Clankelly decimated. The Corrigan's had been fortunate having enough money to afford the rising prices created by the unbridled merchants at times of food shortages. Though Bridget had been born just after the potato blight and Great Famine, which had caused the deaths of over one million Irish people and another million to emigrate, her father could see the writing on the wall for those who remained in their blighted homeland. Sadly those who could leave had, especially the youth. Thus their community was becoming a refuge of the elderly, poor, unemployable and lazy. The prospects for his daughters were poor, suitable husbands were far and few between. Though not wanting to lose them, deprived of their company and solace, he had no choice but to actively encourage all his children to seek a better life. He had come to realise that both the law and social tradition that existed for land subdivision, with all sons inheriting equal shares in a farm, was a recipe for disaster. It meant that farms had become so small they could only grow one crop, potato. A crop failure meant death. As a stone mason, the poor economic conditions had also resulted in Paugeen finding work challenging. Many of the estates, where work should be found, were poorly run by absentee landlords and in many cases heavily mortgaged. He was also worried about the country's political stability and thus the safety of his family. In 1858 the Irish Republican Brotherhood, also known as Fenians, had been founded. This was a secret society dedicated to armed rebellion against the British. Paugeen knew this would result in conflict; religion would become a flashpoint.

When Bridget arrived in Melbourne she found a rapidly growing city that offered a range of opportunities, and soon gained employment as a servant in a suburb called Carlton. This elevated land had been named after the residence of the Prince of Wales. Carlton was part of a large tract of land that surrounded the original town grid of Melbourne and had been set aside in 1839 by the then superintendent, Charles La Trobe. Over time it was sold off for subdivisions, for the development of various public institutions and as public parks, including Carlton Gardens.

Bridget's employers lived in Rathdowne Street, in a large house with front road access and also a carriage lane at the rear allowing access to stables. Bridget had admired several similar homes in the street, but there were also many cottages that had resulted from speculators subdividing blocks creating narrow streets and narrower lanes. The only form of public transport available was horse drawn vehicles but Bridget loved her weekly trip with the cook into the Queen Street meat and fruit markets. She was amazed by the variety of produce, so many types of fruit, vegetables and fish she had never seen. Also the quantity, so much food, truly this was a blessed land.

Though her employers were English, they considered religion a cornerstone of morals so Bridget was allowed to attend mass at St Francis Catholic Church, on the corner of Lonsdale and Elizabeth Street in the centre of the city. It was here that she first noted a well-dressed young man, sitting on the front lawn of the church. He was reading to his companions from *The Argus*, a Melbourne daily morning newspaper. His lifting brogue was unmistakable, full of flowering, musical intonations. She thought him *fear dathuil* with masses of auburn hair protruding from under his straw boater encircled by an emerald green ribbon. She hoped to see him on her next visit, perhaps even get the courage to say hello, but it was weeks before he appeared again.

The second sighting occurred while she was strolling with the family's nanny and children in the Carlton Garden. His attire was less formal, long pants, open necked shirt and vest. He was still reading, but this time in the shade of a Morton Bay fig. As she walked past, he looked up and said, 'C'mere.' He was still wearing the boater, his eyes matching the gleaming green of the ribbon, the colour both mystical and attractive.

On the 28th of June 1875 they were married by Father Peter O'Meara at St Francis Church. John, as he called himself, had been honest. He had talked about his life in Emerald Hill, a poor area of the city previously known as Canvas Town, and later South Melbourne. He openly told her about his challenges, his limited success so far in making his fortune and his hopes and dreams of one day owning his own farm. He also talked about some of the dangers he had faced and recounted his experience on the Clunes goldfield in 1873. At that time he was one of many unsuccessful miners working for an employer who attempted to introduce Saturday afternoon and Sunday shifts. John, like many of his follow miners, refused to sign the new contract and went on strike. However, he happily signed up to a new miners' organisation called the Clunes Miners' Association.

The employers attempted to break the strike by bringing in Chinese workers. John could remember the cries at public meeting to "drive out the unclean yellow men". The morning they were due to arrive he had been handed an axe; others had clubs and waddies, an Aboriginal war club, as weapons. There was almost an air of a carnival with a brass band playing as hundreds of men and women erected barricades of ploughs, upturned drays, timber and bricks, to prevent the Chinese entering the field. He thought the women were actually worse than the men, as they shouted, cursed and threw stones. The Chinese and their police guard were forced to retreat back to Ballarat.

John smiled at this thought, *'No one really wants them here, even the Victorian colonial government charges ships' captains a poll tax of ten pounds per head for any Chinese passenger they landed. But they got around it, the sneaky buggers simply disembarked in South Australia and walked overland. South Australians didn't care, the Chinese were only interested in the gold fields, so got off the ships and left'.*

Bridget realised that John was a man of strong opinions and empathised with his fellow miners. Personally she had limited contact with any Asians. She had seen a few in the Queen Street markets but they had all been very polite and eager to help.

John also talked about the bushrangers who hid in the bush, waiting to rob prospectors both on the way to the fields or as they returned with their gold dust and nuggets. He related rumours about Mad Dog Morgan, Harry Power and the Kelly Gang, and though he had never had any actual contact, he knew lots of stories of their infamous behaviour that had been the talk of the fields, John quickly adding that many such men were simply victims of circumstance.

'Take Ned Kelly for instance. The eldest son of eight children, son of an Irish convict who died when Ned was only twelve. They were simply a poor selector family trying to survive, downtrodden by the Squattocracy who occupied large tracts of government land, and the Kelly's were also victims of persecution by the Victorian Police. This is no different to what the English have been doing to us Irish for hundreds of years.'

Chapter 3

Joannem, who had anglicised his name to John, had arrived in Port Phillip in 1869, after a voyage of ninety days. The ship, *SS Great Britain*, was carrying 490 passengers. John had also arrived as an unassisted migrant whose trade was shown as a farm labourer who could read and write. His journey had been faster than many as the *SS Great Britain* was an iron hulled, steam powered passenger ship, but still had three masts that allowed her also to use sail. When built in 1845 she was the largest passenger ship in the world, advanced for her time. The four decks provided passengers with cabins, dining and promenade saloons. Compared to the experiences of his future wife, his voyage had been luxurious.

John had grown up on the farm that his father and three others share farmed in Ballyarkane, a town overlooking Castlemaine Harbour. The land was owned by the Baron Ventry, their family seat being at Burnham House, near Dingle. The current baron went by the name Dayrolles Blakeney Eveleigh-de-Moleyns (born Mullins), a surname the family had adopted in 1841 in an attempt to claim to be descended from the medieval Norman de Moleyns family. John saw them simply as a wealthy

Protestant family, who lived off his family's hard work and who called themselves British. They were also Unionist unlike his Irish Nationalist beliefs.

A farm of one hundred and ninety-five acres was considered large, but divided among four families and being rented, and thus with no inheritance, made John desire for more. Being a second son with five brothers he felt himself fortunate when his father had agreed to give him what he considered his share of a future inheritance. Now with money in his pocket John, like so many of his friends, headed off, hopefully to make his fortune in the new world. He had originally planned on sailing to America to take part in the gold rush that had occurred in California, but that had started in 1848, nearly twenty years earlier. Worried that most of the discoveries would have already been made, he changed his mind, boarding a ship headed for the Victorian gold fields in Australia.

John's decision was also influenced by the fact that he had an uncle, who he could vaguely remember, who had immigrated sixteen years earlier to the colonies and had written to his father about "making his fortune in the Bald Hills". John had no idea where these were but his uncle had mentioned frequenting the seven public houses at Tambaroora, west of the mountains in the colony of New South Wales.

On his arrival in Melbourne, he was informed of the current rush to Thornton, with mining activity on the Goulburn River, south-east of a place called Alexandra. He purchased a miner's pick, shovel, pan and was also convinced of the need for a pistol for protection. The age and condition of the one provided made him hope he would never have to use it as it looked as if it might explode and kill him. He also obtained a bed roll and some dried food, then set off on foot, surrounded by hundreds of other hopefuls.

He initially tried panning on the edge of the river. A simple technique to find alluvial gold by scooping up a small amount of gravel then moving the pan in a circular motion, the water "swirling out" the mud, leaving small pebbles and hopefully specks of gold. This proved to have limited success so he purchased a large bucket to try puddling. This involved John shovelling clay into the bucket then adding water and again swirling to dissolve the clay, leaving sand and hopefully gold dust or nuggets. When he moved slightly away from the river's edge, the clay bank became hard like cement, so he would have to use his pick to break off clumps.

The work was hard and in the open sun. His hands blistered and his back ached and though he had also purchased a broad brimmed hat, the heat was oppressive. He was used to hard work, ploughing, planting, harvesting and clearing land on his father's farm, but there it was cool with refreshing, gentle breezes. However, on the goldfields men collapsed around him, their lips cracked, their skin blistering. The number of crosses marking the final resting places seemed to grow daily. Though on the water course, fresh water was scarce and expensive as prospecting turned natural water courses into swirling mud pools.

When he did seek shade the buzzing flies and stinging mosquitoes drove man and beast to distraction.

Nights were cooler, lying under a tree, but sleep was limited and light with the constant fear that another desperate prospector would steal your equipment while you were absent, or worse, attempt to rob you as you slept. To counter this John had become part of a team, a group of other young Irish emigrants, men who worked together and also took shifts protecting each other. There had been violence, fights over a particular claim to a section of the creeks bank, rum driven fights based purely on national background, and fights over the prostitutes who plied their trade in the tent towns that sprung up along the ridges near the waterways. In his first year, John's only fight was with a shop owner who tried to overcharge him for supplies. That had ended in a tussle, his nose bloodied, but no permanent injury except to his pride.

Winters proved too cold to remain on the fields, the snow and freezing winds driving him back to Melbourne. Here, sharing a rented room with three other men from his team, he spent some of their hard earned gains, taking time to physically and mentally recuperate. When available, they also tried to earn the next season's stake, unloading cargo or carting goods. It was during one of these winter breaks that he first saw a pretty young girl coming out of the local Catholic church where he and his three friends had placed themselves, hoping to meet some nice women. The men were fresh from the public bath house and barber, smelling of aftershave and dressed in their recently bought clothes, they made an impressionable sight.

They had planned that each of the four men would select a girl they thought looked nice and have one of the others to follow them to see where they went with the hope they could "accidently" run into them at a future time.

There were at the same time pressures and challenges that faced young Irish men such as John and his friends. There were two types, the "Pushes", street gangs often called "larrikins or "larrikinesses" who demonstrated a contempt for authority and were involved in street crime, and the "Irish Mob" or mafia, who were gaining strength in terms of organised crime engaged in assaults, bribery, extortion and illegal gambling. Several times the latter had attempted to recruit John. Though a farceur and exhibitionist, John was not a fighter. Associated with this was the fear and mistrust from British-born Melbournians about the morality of colonial youth and the self-assurances being demonstrated by the new breed of unskilled workers.

Chapter 4

Land sales had begun in Emerald Hill, on the southern bank of Melbourne's Yarra River in 1852, and the tent city of Canvas Town was replaced with small cottages, many that had been prefabricated overseas in timber and corrugated iron. Following their wedding, it was one of these three-roomed cottages that Bridget and John had made their home. In 1872 Emerald Hill had been proclaimed a town and though not the area where they lived, parts of South Melbourne had become a favoured place of residences for the wealthy. St Vincent Gardens had become Melbourne's best London style residential square.

Bridget's first two children, Mary-Anne and Martin, were born in this small and cramped rented cottage. However, by 1878 Bridget was finding life overwhelming; she'd had enough. The iron roof leaked and the walls were mouldy. The fireplace smoked out the house each time she lit it. Her repeated requests to the owner to fix the problems were ignored; it was time to move.

Bridget had complained to Mrs Murphy who lived next door but got little sympathy. She was a widow with six children, three who worked and helped pay the bills but there were also three younger mouths to feed. They had arrived in Port Phillip from County Cork in 1853, at the height of the gold rush. The port had been filled with tall masted ships, unable to move as their crews had jumped ship and headed in search of gold. The only accommodation they could find was a patched tent in what the locals called Canvas Town. Though as part of their organisation to emigrate they had been carefully packing up all their belongings, the Murphys were forced to leave some trunks abandoned on the Port Phillip wharf as they could not find anyone to cart them, plus there was nowhere to store them. The tent they hired cost them one pound per week but when it rained they were saturated and at other times the swirling sand and dust was intolerable.

As thousands of people arrived each day hoping to head to the goldfields, the city could not cope. On the southern bank of the Yarra River with access over the Prince Bridge, built in 1851 replacing a river punt, tents had been erected in erratic rows that went by English names such as Regent, Bond and Liverpool Street. There were stalls selling every imaginable item, with many of the hopeful emigrants desperate for money selling books, clothing, jewellery, even refreshments and ginger beer. There were even tents for physicians who acted as surgeons, dentists and apothecaries. The Murphys never made it to the goldfield; her husband instead had settled for a job at the Cole's Wharf.

Mrs Murphy could remember the fever-like hysteria that seemed to overtake men at the mention of gold. She recalled hearing that one ship's captain, stranded as his crew all deserted to look for gold, had approached the Colonies governor with a plan that he would employ any prisoner in the local jails who had sea experience. He needed about fifty men and there were nearly two hundred and fifty sailors in prison. He was also offering each man sixty pounds on completion of the journey back to England. The governor agreed but all were shocked when only a handful applied, the rest preferring to complete their sentences and still be near the goldfields.

Not long after, all the residents of Canvas Town received a notice informing them that their permits, as the area was Crown Lands owned by the colonial government, were to expire and that the area had to be cleared by the 31st day of March 1854. This had caused a huge panic but because her husband had his job on the wharves they were able to rent the cottage she still lived in. In terms of a few leaks, Mrs Murphy scoffed and talked about the 1863 floods and of timber houses being broken up and washed away, families still inside.

Though John had spent two years leaving his family in Emerald Hill and spending months at a time searching for the elusive gold, he had very little to show for it. In 1877 Bridget had actually gone with him for three months, surviving on the goldfield at Alexandra, originally called Redgate, about 130 kilometres north-east of Melbourne. Living in a small tent, she earned extra money (paid in the form of gold dust or small nuggets) by washing single miners' clothes and serving hot Irish stew, the meat mainly kangaroo. Each time they moved, the tent, all their possessions and the two young children were loaded into a wheelbarrow and wheeled from site to site.

Besides cooking, washing, making bread, mending clothing, making soap and candles, Bridget also spent part of each day working the cradle. This was not the one that held her two infants but a piece of mining equipment also called the rocker box. As the gold they were searching for was found as fine grains and nuggets in the bottom of riverbeds, John would gather buckets of sand and gravel and tip them into a high sided box. John would then pour water in and Bridget would use a pole like handle, rocking the box, thus separating heavier rocks from gravel then fine grains, hopefully including some gold being caught in a canvas sack at the bottom. Sitting on a sawn-off timber stump, she would rock, singing to her children. Her long box pleat skirt and apron were caked with mud. Her bonnet offered some protection from the sun but little help with the swarms of flies.

There were other women at the diggings, some they called good, those who like her had come to look after their families, and the others called bad. These were women who earned a living in a manner that excluded them from Bridget's circle of contacts. Eventually feeling alone and dejected, Bridget fled back to the relative safety and comfort of Emerald Hill, leaving John to his prospecting.

Regardless, at the beginning of 1879, John's search for gold was abandoned and the family moved to 18 Stanley Street, Richmond, Melbourne. This was a one room wide with hall, single storey, two-bedroom, red brick house. It is here their third child Patrick was born.

Though Bridget liked the house and neighbourhood it was not in walking distance of the city, thus John found it too expensive going into the city's centre each day looking for whatever work he could find. Though he hated the perceived stigma, John had found that being a nightman assured him regular employment. This entailed collecting the sewerage pans from backyard privies and dumping their contents into large tubs on a wagon. Once they finished their collection the tubs were dumped directly into the Yarra River which served as the city's unofficial sewer. This added to the noxious state of the waterway that already had industrial waste from upstream. Slaughterhouses, tallow works, tanneries, glue works, bone mills, wool washers, and soap works were just some of the factories dumping foul black waste directly into the river. Regulations related to hygiene, offensive smells and waste disposal were elementary and poorly enforced. The streets in some parts of the city were no better. People still dumped wastewater and sewerage directly into street gutters, letting gravity take it to the lowest point, sometimes pooling at street intersections. For the poor, especially children, this could prove fatal as cholera, diarrhoea, dysentery and hepatitis were a constant threat. Parasites, body and head lice, worms, scabies, sores and tooth decay were also common.

In 1880 the family had moved again, this time to rented rooms in Little Lonsdale Street on the edge of the growing city centre. Still a dirt lane, the street was notorious for its slums, poverty and prostitution. At the northern end of their street, across Spring Street, stood the Model School. In stark contrast to the small homes and shanty constructions of Little Lonsdale, this 1856 grand Palladian style building had been designed to accommodate 350 students. It had been built by the National Education Board in an attempt to further the case for government schools to compete with the Church-run schools. Behind the school the Carlton Gardens were being developed.

Bridget and John liked taking the children for Sunday afternoon walks in the gardens to get fresh air and exercise. They could see the gardens were only in an early stage of development and were told that up unto a few years earlier the land had been mismanaged and illegally grazed leaving only stunted trees and waterlogged soil. From the gardens the family could see the impressive Gaelic church that had been built in 1855 by the Highlanders of Victoria. The building could hold over 600 but services were in Gaelic, the language of the Scottish emigrants. Though some people might refer to Bridget and John as belonging to the Gaelic culture, their language was actually Gaeilge (Gwalgah).

Another large structure in the same line of sight, but less appealing, was the Benevolent Asylum built with government funds and private donations to house the aged and incurable paupers. Even more impressive was the Wesley Church that had been built 1857–58. At the time the architect, Joseph Reed's competition winning design was claimed to be the finest Methodist church in the world. The site also had a new school.

As a place to live the city of Melbourne was unique. Here in the southern hemisphere was a city larger than most European capitals. In the "gold decade" the city's population had doubled, reaching half a million. Though a city of inequality, money had been poured into lavishly decorated buildings with towers, spires, domes and turrets that seemed to reach for the sky. Every new building seemed to be decorated with cast iron. It was called by some the "iron petticoat" city with over forty foundries melting and casting pig iron bars that arrived as ship ballast.

It was here in the struggles to survive that Elizabeth O'Sullivan was born on the 1st of October 1880. Money being very short, Bridget would cook what they had, John and the boys eating first as they would be the bread winners, Bridget and the girls surviving on what was left, often going to bed hungry. John was always looking at other additional work. Bootblacks were popular but in the 1880s John could count fourteen bootblacks in Bourke Street alone. If his boys had been older there was a good chance they would have ended up scoop boys, paid by the Melbourne City Council to pick up the ever-present piles of horse manure. These fourteen to eighteen year olds were also referred to as broomies and sweepers. The opportunity to have your own fruit and vegetable stalls, especially on Princess Bridge, had been another option but by the 1870s this was predominantly the domain of the Chinese, though this had led to hostility towards foreigners, basically defined as those who were non-British.

The wharves always required navvies and boatmen to load and unload cargo, while an army of carters moved goods further afield. The horse powered lifestyle also generated a host of specialist workers, grooms, stable hands, ostlers, horse breakers, coachmen, saddle makers, coach and carriage makers and blacksmiths. In 1879 work had also become available with a government program to straighten a section of the Yarra River making it parallel with the city grid pattern. The project also entailed the removal of the Yarro Yarro Falls, a natural drop in the river where the fresh water met the tidal ocean water. Regardless, for every position there were dozens of failed miners. Bridget considered herself fortunate; she at least had a husband who was willing and able to work. Many women who had arrived in the colony and were either deserted or widowed, found life exceedingly difficult, living in poverty with some forced into prostitution.

On family walks in Carlton Gardens they watched with interest the building of a new Exhibition Centre. John had been able to get some labourer work on the building that covered about seven acres and measured five hundred by one hundred and sixty feet, cruciform in plan, with a dome sixty feet in diameter that rose two hundred and seventeen feet above the building. Under the dome, the words "Victoria Welcomes All Nations" were written.

Being seen as a keen worker, John was also asked to help set up some of the displays.

Though entry to the Melbourne International Exhibition was expensive, workers were provided with free passes so John was excited to take Bridget and the children to see the wonders on display. While working on the site he had heard others talking in disgusted tones how Sydney, considering themselves the first and major city and knowing of Melbourne's plans, had quickly thrown together an exhibition, the Sydney International Exhibition of October 1879. Later there was mirth when the workers heard that as the Sydney exhibition focused mainly on agriculture, it did not meet the criteria for official recognition, thus Melbourne's would be the first International Exhibition in Australia, running from October 1880 to April 1881. At the time the exhibition building was the largest in Australia and the tallest in Melbourne.

John's family were amazed at the displays from eighteen nations and twenty-one colonies. He sampled tea in the Ceylonese section, cocoa in the Dutch and beer in the Austrian pavilion. In the United States pavilion he was fascinated with the new agricultural machinery but also the barbed wire, electric light, and an early version of a mechanical lawn mower. Victoria had its own specialities including a full-size locomotive from the Phoenix Foundry of Ballarat. The exhibition had been open several months before John took his family to see the displays, but they had previously been among the 100,000 in the main thoroughfares of the city the day the exhibition was to open. He had seen a fleet of ships in the bay, ablaze with colourful bunting. The trade societies had mustered strongly, their members dressed in their best clothing marching behind silken banners. The Naval Brigade, Fire Brigade and police all paraded. People cheered as His Excellency the Governor entered the building to be greeted by a choir of ladies in white dresses and a band. John also saw many town mayors and aldermen entering in their official robes. Most of the ladies and gentlemen, in what appeared to be an official party, were in evening costume. John noticed the Royal Standard being hoisted over the dome and as it was a canon salute was fired from several ships and shore batteries.

John constantly struggled to find work but as if by miracle, an answer to Bridget's prayers, he received a letter in 1882 from a relative who was setting up a dairy farm, south of the Cooks River, at a place called Botany in the colony of New South Wales. The area had become viable when new all-weather roads and permanent river crossings had been established allowing farm products to be taken to the Sydney markets. His older, single uncle was of the belief that relatives would make the most honest and reliable workers, plus as he was planning on only offering them food and board with the possibility of inheritance, they would also be the cheapest solution.

Chapter 5

John eagerly priced tickets on the railway from Melbourne to Sydney. Even though the two colonies had built their rail with different gauges it had been possible from 1881 to change trains at Albury, at the border, to reach Sydney. Prior to this, railway focus had been on moving people and goods from coastal ports to inland communities as ships met the needs of inter-colony transport with passengers and goods having to pass through intercolonial customs and immigration at borders. It would not be till federation of the colonies in 1901, and the introduction of free trade, that standard gauge would become an issue. The Victorian colony had built their rail as a broad gauge five feet three inches and the New South Wales colony and South Australian colony both adopted standard gauge four feet eight and a half inches. At the same time the colony in Queensland built their rail with narrow gauge of three feet six inches. Though rail would have been the fastest option, it was too expensive. John's other option was a coastal trip; thus as steerage passengers on the iron screw coastal steamer *Arawata*, part of the Blue Emu line, they sailed north to a new life.

They discovered on arrival that there was no home on the block which had previously been used for grazing and had strands of timber removed for lumber to be used for roof shingles, railway sleepers, firewood and to make charcoal. While John worked on the farm, living initially in a tent, the family had to live in a series of rented houses in the inner city. Their child Daniel was born in Marrickville in 1883, Maggie in 1884 in Botany, John in 1885 in St Peters, twins Bridget and Dennis in 1888 in Newtown, but both died in their first few months and Elsie in 1890, also at the rented home in Newtown.

Initially Bridget had been pleased with this inner city living as she had read that the Reverend James Hassell, curate of St Peter's Cooks River, had described the district where the farm was located as "the wildest and godless a place as he had ever known". Though they had nearly vanished it had been the home of the "Cabbage Tree Hat Mob". These sawyers, who made their living from sawing wood, were known for organising bare-knuckle boxing bouts, cockfights, and dog fights in secluded clearings in the forest. However, there was another side to the area and John had taken Bridget to see "The Warren". This was a thirty-room stone gothic mansion that had been built in 1857 overlooking the Cooks River by a business tycoon, Thomas Holt. Holt gave it the name Warren because he imported and bred rabbits on the estate for hunting. Holt encouraged school children and common people to visit his estate in an attempt to educate them on his artworks and sculptures plus to be impressed by his landscaped gardens and exotic animals such as alpaca. Though not open to the public, John had also shown her Canterbury House. Also overlooking the river this rustic gothic residence featured a spectacular circular drive with enormous gardens, a lodge house, orangery and carriage road lined with pine trees.

Eventually a dwelling was constructed on the dairy and the family moved in, but it was a hard life for the older children, now having to work long hours on the farm. Though Bridget cooked and cleaned, she was weakened by the birth of the twins and another child less than two years later, thus Mary, aged sixteen, had to care for two sisters and four brothers. Martin aged fourteen and Patrick, twelve, oversaw the milking and Elizabeth, eleven, Daniel, nine and Maggie, seven were tasked with rounding up the cows, morning and night. The uncle allowed the family to grow vegetables, consume as much dairy as they liked and have chooks for fresh eggs, but money was still in short supply, so the children went bare footed.

A favourite story in later life told of warming up feet in winter by stepping in fresh cow pats. The children also gathered leaves from the cabbage-tree palms which grew in the creek gullies. These were woven into hats and were exceedingly popular; the best could be sold for several guineas each. John handled the milk deliveries till Patrick was old enough to take it over. By then Martin was away working with horses and Elizabeth had become the family debt collector. School for the older children was very limited, a secondary consideration.

John was concerned how the area continued to change. Market gardens had been developed on the rich alluvial flats near Muddy Creek, Nobbs Flat and along the creeks that flowed into the Cooks River. Larger holdings were being broken up with more intensive farming of potatoes, corn and melons, crops that would survive the rough wagon trip to the Sydney's markets. These wagons often returned loaded with food scraps from Sydney's restaurants that allowed pig and poultry farmers to fatten their livestock. Large parcels of land were being subdivided and sold off as the city encroached on the available rural lands. A further trend John found worrying, following his experiences in the goldfields, was the number of Chinese who started renting the land along the river for their gardens.

John's extended Irish family in Australia grew with the arrival of his brother Daniel in 1881 via two years in New Zealand. Daniel was twelve years younger than John and was only eight years old when John left for the British colony of New South Wales. Daniel visited the family in Melbourne but travelled on to Sydney where he obtained employment in a brick making yard till he too went in search of gold, but in his case at Boulder Gold mines, Kalgoorlie in the Western Australian colony. He, however, was successful in his prospecting and purchased a wheat and sheep property near Pingelly in Western Australia. After several years his family moved back to New South Wales where they bought a dairy property at Bocca Creek on the state's north coast, near Coffs Harbour. Daniel also established a carrying business using horses and wagons, partly contracted to carry goods from the railhead to the Fitzroy Hotel in Coffs Harbour.

Chapter 6

Though life for Bridget and John was a constant challenge, it was in the context of a country and world heading into crisis. The 1880s had seen a period of economic boom in the colony. For the O'Sullivan's, this activity encouraged Bridget to again set up her laundering business, providing a steady income as the number of single men working in the wharf areas and renting shared rooms created a steady supply of customers. While John was working at Botany, Bridget, between childbearing and care, also did some cleaning and cooking at one of the local hotels, her daughter Mary-Anne, though still a child herself, being left to care for her younger siblings. The demand for cheap housing in the inner city saw it outstrip supply. Developers opted for very high-density housing which led to rows and rows of terrace houses being built. Many called for a halt to this type of approaching slum development, citing crime and disease.

Bridget did feel that the natural landscape of the city was under attack. Bushland was rapidly being replaced by concrete and bitumen, surrounded by brick and tiles. Sandstone hillsides had been hacked to pieces, dissected and levelled to create usable land for factories and houses as well as provide stone for buildings. Reclamation of the harbour foreshore had reduced access and the harbour itself was shrinking. Parts of the city had also become unsafe. By 1891, the area of Surry Hills along Riley, Oxford and Liverpool Streets had become a notorious slum area known as the Robin Hood Lane area. It contained 776 houses which housed over 2,500 people who Bridget would call the undesirables.

There was also Frog Hollow, an area on Riley and Reservoir Streets, a notorious criminal area. This was a maze of dirt lanes and ramshackle homes on top of each other. The criminal element ran the sly grog shops, cocaine distribution and prostitution. Street gangs called Pushes terrorised anyone who they felt had no business to be in the area.

Though John felt politically isolated on the farm, he still tried, whenever he could get a copy of *The Bulletin* magazine, to read in candlelight from cover to cover, to keep up with the news. It was a Sydney publication that John had first read after they arrived in their new life. Initially published in 1880, the magazine focussed on politics and business. John loved the cartoons and illustrations that accompanied some of the articles. He felt it reflected his attitudes on what this society should be like: nationalistic, pro-labour and pro-republican. One of his favourite contributors was Henry Lawson with his first published piece in the 1st of October 1887 edition, a poem, *Song of the Republic*. His phrases like "Those old-world errors and wrongs and lies", and "And free from the wrongs of the North and Past. The land belongs to you", resonated with his beliefs, for homeland Ireland and new land, Australia. He noted that Lawson had not referred to either the British Empire or Australia by name, something he thought his brothers in Ireland needed to learn. If you wrote to deliberately spark rebellion, then you could be convicted of treason and as the Australian colonies were still under British control, that was a real risk. John equally enjoyed Lawson's follow up pieces such as *Faces in the Street* in 1888, *The Hymn of the Socialist* in 1889 and *Songs of the Outcast*, the first telling of the poor's misery, the filthy lanes and cruel, heartless streets. The others expounded on the poverty facing many in society, calling for the downtrodden to strike when the time comes.

He had read up on the writer and felt empathy, perhaps more, for his father a Norwegian-born sailor who had jumped ship to join the gold rushes. Like his own family, the Lawsons (Larsen) moved often in search of gold. Like John he had not been successful and had to settle, in his case taking up a selection in marginal country. Both had to take whatever building work they could find to make a living. Like his wife Bridget, Louisa Lawson was often lonely and vulnerable with her husband's absences; she also had demanded better and they had also moved to Sydney. John found Henry Lawson's writing deeply humane with no romantic or idyllic imagery, just accurate descriptions of what the average emigrant would face in this vast, harsh land. It was another piece in *The Bulletin* of 1892 that John considered Lawson's most profound.

This was a short story called *The Drover's Wife*. John considered it to reflect what Bridget and many women who had emigrated had to face and be, strong but often lonely women who tried to run family farms and businesses while raising children with their husbands away. Through these heroines facing constant challenges, Lawson used imagery to question gender stereotyping.

In 1890 the catalyst for industrial action hinged on the employers attempting to break the increasing power and solidarity of the union movement and their longstanding claims over pay and conditions. The maritime dispute of that year quickly spread from the seamen to wharf labourers, then gas stokers and coal miners. Coal miners from Newcastle and Broken Hill were locked out after refusing to dig coal for non-union operated vessels. At the same time the Amalgamated Shearers' Union of Australia issued a manifesto calling on a boycott of non-union shorn wool. The government of the day used military units to support the police and help break up meetings and strikes.

There were signs of a greater threat with sixteen small banks and building societies collapsing in Melbourne, causing the loss of many families' savings. The first major bank to fail was the Bank of Van Diemen's Land in 1891. By the end of the year it was estimated that half of the Australian bank customers were not able to access their accounts. By 1893 the government of Victoria implemented a five day bank holiday to ameliorate the panic and runs on the banks. For Bridget, banks and accounts were not an issue; she had a special place to keep spare cash not trusting the institutions of the upper classes. However, with the strikes and lockouts, men could no longer afford the luxury of having someone wash their clothing and as the patronage of the hotel fell that work also dried up. With the ever-increasing number of men wandering the streets of the city, even some banging on their front door asking for any work or any spare food, she was pleased to move to the rural tranquillity and isolation of the farm.

Bridget had received letters from friends in Melbourne and conditions there seemed far worse. They told of relief societies being set up to distribute bread, meat, tea, sugar and fuel, and the dehumanising feeling of having to get a "ticket" denoting their needy status. She bemoaned those men who remained too proud to accept charity, their wives and children, weak and dressed in rags, queuing up to accept the handouts. Bridget was also distressed by stories she read in their local papers telling that over a third of Melbourne's breadwinners were out of work and one in ten Melbourne houses had been repossessed by the banks.

One of her last recollections as she and the children were packing to leave their rented home in Newtown was hearing bells and yelling, people heading towards the city. She saw their local fire brigade with its horse drawn cart of water tank, hose and ladders moving quickly in the same direction. The spectacle was a large fire that destroyed buildings between Castlereagh, Moore and Pitts Street that were valued at 750,000 pounds sterling. The fire had engulfed a full city block, almost a hectare, including a large number of warehouses and office buildings.

John was faced with a real conflict in 1893 when gold was discovered at Kalgoorlie, Western Australia. He was desperate to go, and spent days speculating on options. His uncle had recently died so the farm had been signed over to him. To leave risked the work of ten years, but it was Bridget who stopped him in his tracks; she was not going to drag her family to the other side of the continent; she would not be there if he left her alone again. Sadly the decision resulted in John suffering from persistent feelings of sadness and loss. He constantly complained of pains, lack of energy and thus his sons were forced to take on most of the physical roles John had previously performed on the dairy.

Chapter 7

Elizabeth left the farm at the age of twenty to work as a maid in the boarding house owned by her married older sister, Mary-Anne. Though strenuous work, she enjoyed the interaction with the guests, most of whom were young, single men, who worked on the docks. The majority were northern European, Swedish, Norwegian and some Germans. As most of her family were short to average height, the boarders all seemed to be tall, physically strong and generally easy going.

Though she wouldn't admit it, her favourite time of the day was when the men returned from work, and in the back yard, stripped to the waist to wash off coal soot or dust before putting on a clean shirt and enter the dining room for their evening meal. One of Elizabeth's jobs was to wash the men's clothing, another to carry hot water from the back yard laundry copper to the washing basins. The men knew she was there, half hiding behind the laundry door. Some would pose, stretching muscular shoulders, but one, a Swede, would flick water in her direction, always with a warm smile and cheeky grin on his face. Of the guests, he seemed to have the best understanding of

English and tended to use it, while the others mainly conversed to each other in their native tongues.

Being the landlady's sister, Elizabeth was sure they showed her a little more respect than some of the other maids. The tall Swede was named Carl Carlsson and he called this happy energetic girl Busy Lizzie and soon everyone in the boarding house referred to her as Lizzie. In return she called him Charlie Boy, a name that also stuck with Carl for the rest of his life. Lizzie had chosen this nickname as to her it summed up this tall, foreigner. He seemed so gentle and certainly had the gift of storytelling, and even with his broken English, he could mesmerise others when he elaborated on a truth. Lizzie also found him inquisitive and genuinely interested in the answers she gave when questioned. She had also called him Charlie as he reminded her of a character from a book her father loved and often read to them from. Charles Darnay was an impressive character in Charles Dickens' 1859 novel, *A Tale of Two Cities*: "A young man of about five-and-twenty, well-grown and well-looking, with a sunburnt cheek and a dark eye". In the tale he also exhibits an admirable honesty and courageousness.

One day Charlie asked her about her father's name and when she told him he laughed, 'So you are really Lizzie Joannemsdotter, not O'Sullivan.' Having a quick temper she snapped back about how silly it was that all Swedes kept changing their names for each generation. This led to one of their first long conversations sitting in the small back garden under the shady foliage of a Morton

Bay fig tree. Though he had never heard the term patronymics (from the Greek pater, meaning father, and onoma for name) he tried to explain about the use of "son" and "dotter" in naming. To Lizzie it was just strange; she wondered how you would ever really know who your family were. Charlie was a Carlsson but his grandfather an Andersson, great grandfather an Olofsson then, Ersson, even an Udsson and so on.

Charlie naturally asked about O'Sullivan and Lizzie was pleased she could remember bits of the story her father had told her about where their name came from. Though she had little formal education and struggled to read and write, she had a quick and retentive mind.

'It was the year nine hundred and fifty in Ireland and the chief of a local clan named Eochuid McMaoiliora was with his family and friends being entertained by a well-known Scottish druid, Lu Vane, with his poems. It was custom to give entertainers gifts, thus as he was leaving Eochuid asked him what he desired. Lu Vane, who was a cruel man, stated that nothing would satisfy him but the left eye from the host's head. Having already lost the sight of his right eye during a battle, Eochuid considered this an inhuman and brutal request. However, to maintain his pride and fame for never refusing anything he had the power to grant, he thrust his finger into his eye and removed it. Upon learning about his great personal sacrifice, a holy man, Ruan Lorha immediately came to the castle. With Eochuid's wife and friends they prayed that Lu Van's fair eyes would be removed and go to Eochuids.

Their prayers were answered and Eochuid's descendants took the name Suile-Luvane meaning the eyes of Lu Vane.'

Charlie had to agree that the tale about her name was far more interesting. He knew little of his own personal history, some names and places, but his strongest memories were of the tales of Galma Uppsala, the home of the legendary Yngling Dynasty, that his mother Brita has told him during the long dark winters of his childhood and from his Uncle Ulf while working on his farm.

From their first few conversations the one thing that Charlie picked up on very quickly was Lizzie's dislike, perhaps even hatred, of the English. Related to her tale of being O'Sullivan, her father had instructed his children on how the English army had driven the O'Sullivan clan out of County Tipperary in 1193. Resettling in County Kerry they were again driven out, this time by the armies of Oliver Cromwell in 1654. The clan had been ordered to move into the wastelands of County Clare where there was "not wood enough to hang a man, not water enough to drown him and not earth enough to bury him". Though the O'Sullivans had been dispossessed of their lands her family had stayed in the hills above Castlemaine Harbour, County Kerry. As long as they were willing to pay rent to an English lord, for what used to be their own land, they could stay. She explained that her grandfather, Martini O'Sullivan, leased his land from Lord Ventry but as Martini had seven children her father had left Ireland for the gold fields of Australia in hope of making his fortune.

The younger sister of Mary-Anne and Elizabeth, Maggie also went to work in the Margaret Street boarding house. Like her sister Lizzie, she also married one of the seamen boarders, a Swede by the name of Gustave Wilhelm Carlsson from Gothenburg. They were married in 1904 at St Patrick's Catholic Church, Millers Point.

Chapter 8

A new land and new life

Carl Carlsson had arrived in Sydney at the end of 1898. At twenty-seven he had lost his love for the challenges of the sea; though he never thought it could happen, he rationalised that his future lay on the land. He had family here, his brother Anders was living in The Rocks, an area near the wharves, but his house was small and he had four children. Anders, having received a letter from Carl who was recuperating in Fremantle, had managed to organise both a job on the wharves and a place for Carl to live. On the ships Carl had been a coal lumper so Anders felt that he would be suited to, and accept, the work required to fit into the coal community.

The boarding house where his older brother Anders had organised a room was located at 9 Margaret Street between Kent and York Street. Anders knew the proprietor, John Sandy, who was also of Swedish background. He had left Sweden as Johan Erik Kragsterman but when he arrived in Newcastle anglicised his name. He took the name Sandy because the men on his ship had called him that as he had white, sandy coloured hair. He had travelled to Sydney where he met and married an Irish lass, Mary-Anne O'Sullivan. While Mary-Anne ran their boarding house, John, a Master mariner, was working on the Sydney ferries. In 1909 he was made the captain of the *Carrabella*, a ferry on the Circular Quay to Mosman run and owned by the Port Jackson Steamship Company.

Mary-Anne, from 1906 to 1908, also had a shop at 30 and 1/2 Kent Street. She had set it up to try and support the large number of seamen boarding in the area. Basically it was hot meals served in tin dishes that the seamen carried. In 1911 when John died, Mary Sandy, with her five young children, moved to North Sydney where she bought a small business, calling it Mrs Sandy's Ham and Beef.

Chapter 9

The Shipwreck, 1887

It seemed like only a moderate southerly gale and he had sailed in far worse conditions. The *Villalta* was running down the coast close hauled on the starboard tack under topsails, fore and main course. The seas were fresh and the ship's bow was dipping under the waves. The second officer, Francis Cox, reported to the captain that there was land abeam but Captain Harland did not believe him. Harland had been on deck all night and though he had enjoyed a few warming rums, he was confident in his calculations. He was sure Cox's sighting was just the patches of moonlight flashing between clouds, reflecting off the waves. A few minutes later Hilmar Tibet, a Norwegian crew member who was on watch called out, seeing a breaker.

The first touch of the reef was gentle enough; the *Villalta* lurched to starboard but righted itself though water washed over the deck. It was 12.45 a.m. and Carl was asleep in his hammock. He rolled out only to be thrown to the lower deck as a wave drove the barque hard onto the Leschenant Reef. Waves were now breaking over the screaming hull, the noise drowning out the orders being yelled by the captain. Carl was glad the *Villalta* was a relatively new ship, having been built in Glasgow fourteen years earlier in 1883. Its strong hull of riveted steel provided greater protection than many of the earlier ships he had crewed on, these being constructed of timber.

Carl struggled to keep his footing as the ship bucked with each attacking wave. He used both muscular hands to haul himself up the rope that acted as a handrail support on the steps to the upper deck. As he emerged into the cold dark night another wave smashed onto the raised quarterdeck. He heard the pounding of the cargo, sounding like it also was trying to escape the reality of a ship breaking apart.

The three masted *Villalta* had left Tacoma in Puget Sound in America on 9th of November 1896 with a crew of eighteen and a cargo of timber for Fremantle, Western Australia. Carl had sailed in these waters before as a crew member on the barque *New Market* in 1892 when he had also visited his brother, a fellow sailor who now lived in Sydney on the east coast in the colony of New South Wales. However, on this trip the first Australian land sighted had been Hautman Rock, to the north of the Abrolhos, four days before the wreck. This is a chain of one hundred and twenty-two islands and associated coral reefs, in the Indian Ocean off the west coast of the Australian mainland. The captain knew of the dangers of the area with its many shipwrecks, the most famous being the Dutch ships *Batavia* in 1629 and the *Zeewijk* in 1727.

Captain Harlan had read the accounts of the *Batavia*, a ship carrying 341 passengers, forty of whom drowned trying to get to shore, then a further one hundred and twenty-five (men, women, children and infants) who were massacred by others who mutinied. The captain of the *Batavia* had sailed for help in a long boat, heading for the Dutch East India colony at Batavia, leaving a merchant, Jeronimus Cornelisz, in charge. Arriving back with a rescue party four months later, and faced with the realisation of what had happened in his absence, the captain had Cornelisz and six others executed, the first Europeans executed in Australia. The other ship, the *Zeewijk*, was also well documented and Captain Harland remembered that on that occasion, of the 208 on the ship at the time of the wreck, 82 had survived by building a second boat out of the debris of the *Zeewijk* and sailing it to Batavia, reaching their destination ten months after the wreck. Batavia, also known as the Queen of the East and Jewel of the East, was a port in the Indonesian archipelago. Its harbour was on the Ciliwang River, abuzz with merchant vessels from Europe, China, India and Arab areas. Its warehouses were stacked with exotic spices, tin and copper. The original Dutch fort had been replaced by a trading centre in 1619 and named Batavia after the ancestors of the Dutch, the Batavieren.

From the Arbrothos islands the *Villalta* had beat down the coast on the same tack for twenty-four hours. At five o'clock the captain calculated the vessel's position to be about fifty miles off land, and expected to sight the rotating light of Rottnest Island, the largest and northern most of several islands nineteen kilometres (twelve miles) from Fremantle. The Wadjemup Lighthouse had been built on Rottnest in 1849. A twenty metre (66 feet) limestone tapered cylindrical tower with balcony and lantern, it had been built to provide a safer sailing passage for ships arriving at Fremantle Port and the Swan River Colony. Though an experienced captain who had safely guided them through the South China Sea, Captain Harlan had not sailed in Australian waters and was unaware of the strong ocean currents that were driving his vessel to disaster.

With waves breaking over the vessel, it very quickly became obvious that there was no chance of saving the ship. Carl heard the captain's frantic voice ordering the longboat lowered. Carl was a strong swimmer and grabbed a lifebelt but the slings had perished with age and snapped. He and three other crew were ordered into the lifeboat and to keep her off the ship's side. Though the waves tossed them like a cork they managed to keep the small boat secured enough for the others to climb down, the captain, the last, after having put the ship's papers into the pillowcase and thrown it down to Carl. Harland gave the order to, 'Man the oars and keep her head up to the sea,' but she got beam on and capsized. All eighteen crewmen were tossed into the swirling foam.

Carl managed to cling onto the upturned boat but the young apprentice, William Thomas, vanished under a wave, his life belt also disintegrating. William, who could not swim, tried to survive by holding onto another crew member's leg, but in an act of self-preservation he had been kicked away. It took the crew about twenty minutes to right the lifeboat as in doing so it had turned over three times. The frantic men worked together and as the clouds scattered they were rewarded with intermittent moonlight.

Debris filled the water as the sea washed the cargo, some of the timber having been stacked on the top deck and all other moveable items away. The barque now lay on her beam with the deck facing seaward, about four kilometres offshore. The force of the sea battered the remaining timber cargo below deck and timber was beginning to protrude through the ship's steel hull like spears killing the wounded beast. One by one the men hauled themselves onto the lifeboat, sixteen in total. Captain Harland had vanished. The oars had been washed away, so the men broke up the lining and bottom boards to use as makeshift paddles allowing them to finally reach the shore at about eight o'clock in the morning. The temperature was already climbing; the arid blistering heat of a southern hemisphere summer was to be their next challenge. Barely saving themselves, they had no food or water.

With no signs of human habitation and not knowing where they had landed, Second Officer Cox decided they should head south, toward their original destination, following the rocky desert-like shoreline. The terrain was harsh and the temperature relentless. Desperation was replaced by despair with three of the crew dying from dehydration and heat stroke related symptoms. Several of the men had jumped into the longboat without shoes; fortunately Carl had slipped his on as the burning sand blistered raw skin. On the fourth day, as the thirteen remaining crew huddled in the shade of a large boulder for protection, fortune swung in their favour. They were found by some stockmen from the Coobarby cattle station.

The first face Carl saw was of a man under a broad brimmed hat, white shining teeth in an otherwise black face. He couldn't understand what he was saying but his smile was reassuring. There were three other men, one with the same dark complexion and masses of curly black hair and two with brown, sun tanned skin but light brown hair who were speaking English to Officer Cox. The survivors were taken to the nearby town of Gin Gin where another two died. There wasn't much at Gin Gin—a police station, railway station and a few dwellings—but a telegraph line linking to Perth allowed details of the wreck to be sent and help requested.

Though Carl had fared better than most of his companions he felt tired and weak all the time. He had tried to follow the instructions given by the stockmen, small sips of water and small quantities of food, but his movement was greatly reduced by severe joint and leg pain. His shins were a mess of red and blue spots and every bump seemed to bruise. After four days his sun cracked lips had swollen, his gums bleeding. The plan by the local police constable was to allow the now eleven surviving men to recuperate then put them on a train to Perth.

On receiving the telegram, the Adelaide Steamship Co. Ltd had immediately sent their steamship *Colac* to the wreck site and instructions were given to move Carl and the others to the mouth of the nearby Moore River for them to be transferred by long boat to another British ship, the *Prins Vladimar*, and taken to Fremantle. The officers on the *Prins Vladimar* had seen many cases of scurvy and immediately started Carl on a course of lemon juice.

Now finally sailing past the island called Rottnest, Carl watched as sea lions and fur seals played on the white sand beaches and secluded coves of what appeared to be a sandy low-lying island. Carl asked one of the other sailors did the island have lots of rats, as that was how he heard the name. Stefan, also a Swede but who had made many coastal voyages along the Australian coast and spoke both Swedish and good English, explained that small rat-like animals did live there but they were actually quokka. They were a plant eating animal with a long tail that moved around by hopping on their back legs. Carl said he had seen an animal like that when they had been in Gin-Gin. The people there had called them kangaroo but they were as tall as a man.

Stefan explained there were many types, 'Like the deer at home, with our large elk and moose, the smaller reindeer and even smaller roe deer. As we hunt the deer for food here the local dark skinned people, the Aborigines, hunt kangaroo both for food and wear their skins as a coat I have heard called a Buka.'

Carl had also seen some of these people in Gin-Gin and also with the stockmen that had found them but could not understand them as they seemed to speak in their own language. Stephan called them the Noongar people who were here long before the arrival of white men, explaining that these people seemed to be from many different tribes each with their own language.

Fremantle as a port consisted of a long jetty that extended into the open sea. Carl could see that the mouth of the river that met the ocean had its estuary blocked by a rocky bar. He heard the officers complaining that the jetty offered no shelter and the strong south-westerly winds battered the ship against the wooden pier. He watched the cargo being unloaded and with it he headed down Cliff Street in Fremantle's west end. Though he was to stay in Fremantle, the cargo was loaded onto barges that sailed up the Swan River to Perth, the capital of the Swan River colony.

Major construction was taking place to change the port and he watched the dredging on the rock bar creating a channel. They were also constructing two massive moles, stone breakwaters to protect the new entrance. He noted signs of land reclamation where he assumed a new quay and warehouses would be built.

After disembarking at Fremantle, the men from the *Villalta* were moved to a sailors' mission where Carl was to spend over a month slowly regaining his strength but with the loss of much of his thick curly black hair. Finding himself a witness at the enquiry into the wreck that resulted in Captain Harland being held responsible for the wreck because of careless navigation, he was saddened as he liked Harland and thought him a good sober captain. He understood that such a finding against a dead man cleared the name and reputations of the other two officers and therefore, under Section 2 51 Vic, No. 6, all proceedings in the matter ceased. Carl had heard that Harland had only recently married in America and his wife had sailed a few weeks after them to meet her husband in Sydney.

While spending five weeks recovering in the mission, Carl obtained employment at a warehouse that stored bales of wool waiting for shipment. As he was weakened by his ordeal, the owner initially gave him, in return for a cot, food and some spending money, light work such as moving ropes and tackles. Carl was fascinated by the fact that Daniel had arrived in the colony a convict. It had been thirty years earlier but here he was a free and wealthy man. He had arrived on the ship *Hougoumont* in 1868 as one of sixty-two Fenian political prisoners, transported for their part in the Fenian Rising, a rebellion by the Irish Republican Brotherhood against British rule in Ireland. Like Daniel, many of his fellow convicts were educated and literate to the extent that during the voyage a number of the Fenians entertained themselves by producing seven editions of a shipboard newspaper entitled *The Wild Goose*.

This group of convicts was a further breach of the agreement between the Western Australian colony and Britain. When established in 1828 the colony at Swan

River was advertised as a free settlement and this had proved attractive to many potential settlers. Over time they realised that the other colonies had a large source of basically free labour in the form of convicts, thus the Swan River Colony found it could not compete in pricing to sell their products or in the development of much needed capital works. Karl Marx, in *Das Kapital*, used the Swan River Colony to illustrate a point re the necessity of a dependent workforce for capitalist production and colonisation. Daniel knew of both his works, *The Communist Manifesto* of 1848 and *Das Kapital* of 1867 to 1883. For Daniel, a workers' revolt against the upper classes and landlords was the solution for Ireland, not his new home.

Although taking a small number of juvenile offenders from 1842, it was not a formally constituted penal colony till 1849. The juveniles were required to apprentice themselves to local tradesmen and when they did were given their freedom. The community had placed three restrictions on its convict intake: no female convicts, no political prisoners and no convicts convicted of serious crime. Though no female convicts were transported to Western Australia the other two limitations were ignored. However, nearly forty percent of the convicts arriving in Western Australia were classified as artisans and over sixty percent semiliterate or literate and nearly seventy percent under the age of thirty. The other consideration was that the majority had almost finished their prison sentence and were looking to become free men. These percentages were much higher than other penal colonies and provided a skilled and relatively well-educated labour supply.

Daniel had adapted from resentment to realisation of the opportunities this forced emigration had given him. His passion for the cause had not dwindled but his drive for a better life took over. Upon gaining his freedom he had worked hard, married and raised a large family, all of whom were educated and three with their own businesses. Now in his late fifties, he allowed his son to run the warehouse but was there each day, a local newspaper in hand, just checking. Daniel was happy to share his paper with Carl, reading sections he thought Carl might find interesting and also helping Carl to improve both his writing and reading of English. Daniel was a *Herald* man, and was proud that the paper, first published as a weekly in 1867, was owned by James Pearce, William Beresford and James Roe, all ex-convicts like himself. The *Herald* also supported social reform, something close to his own heart. Daniel also read *The West Australian* but considered it to have conservative leanings.

Daniel found in Carl a good listener. Unlike most young men he was not rushing off in search of gold. They enjoyed their evening rum together and Carl accompanied Daniel on his evening inspections of the wharves and ship arrivals, as a companion but also a bodyguard. It wasn't going to hurt having an over six foot Swede carrying a staff with you at night. On these walks Daniel expounded on the importance of having a place you called home and the strength that came from having a family. Though still considering himself Irish, he knew that this new land had given his children a far better lifestyle and greater opportunities than they would have received in the old country.

During his time in Fremantle, Carl saw plans for the construction of two lighthouses at the entrance to the new harbour. The South Mole Lighthouse was to be painted green, starboard or right side, the North Mole in red, port or left side. Though these had not been constructed by the time he left, Carl had been in Fremantle for the opening of the inner harbour on the 4th of May 1897. He watched the first steamer, *Sultan*, drawing just one foot of water with Lady Forrest at the wheel. Her husband, Sir John Forrest, was an Australian explorer and politician. He was the first premier of Western Australia from 1890 to 1901.

Unlike some of his fellow sailors, Carl did not develop the gold fever that had also been a major driver for the development of the Fremantle port. The first gold in Western Australia had been found in 1888 to the north of where Carl had been shipwrecked at a place called the Kimberley but it had been short lived. Another find at Southern Cross, a community 371 kilometres east of the Fremantle port, in a dry desert area, had occurred in 1888. The small town had boomed for a couple of years then declined. The major discovery in 1893 at Mount Charlotte was to become the Kalgoorlie-Boulder gold rush, located 600 kilometres east of the Fremantle port. The once barren bush populated by hopping kangaroos was now filling with masses of humanity.

The population increase had brought wealth to the state and the area had experienced a boom in capital works with roads, railways, and in 1896 the commencement of construction on the Goldfield Water Supply Scheme, a dam near Perth and pipeline to the gold fields. The voices and faces Carl heard and saw pass through his port location included African, British, Americans, South Seas islanders, Chinese and Indian, mostly men, leaving their families in far corners of the world.

Carl found the heat of this south-western Australian city oppressive. His days when not working were put to good use improving his spoken English and learning to read and write in that language. Gas streetlights had been installed in Fremantle by 1887 so it was during the early evenings that he did most of his exercise, walking long distances around the harbour's shoreline.

He was surprised to find that Fremantle and Western Australia as a colony was forbidden from operating its own naval vessels. Having seen some artillery on his walks, he was informed they were manned by a militia unit, known as the Freemantle Naval Artillery, that had been formed to assist in the defence of Fremantle Harbour. The artillery unit was made up of ex-Royal Navy men and merchant seamen of good character. This made Carl smile; very few of the seamen he had met, naval or merchant, had good character. Some were certainly courageous, most loyal and caring, at least to their fellow shipmates, but the traits of integrity, honesty and good morals were perhaps grey areas.

In late November 1897 Carl felt well enough to sign on as crew for a coastal vessel bound for Sydney and his brother Anders.

Chapter 10

Anders Gustaf Carlsson was the second child of Carl Andersson and Brita Christina Larsdotter. They had married in 1859 in Vaddo, Stockholm, Sweden, when both were aged twenty-two. Brita had managed to get permission from her father to marry, as up till 1870, women in Sweden could not marry without permission from their father or legal guardian.

Her father, Lars Ersson, was a stableman in Hammarby, Edebo, Stockholm. At the time of their marriage Brita was a maid servant at Borntorp and Anders had finished serving five years in the Swedish Navy, based at Karlskonka, an ice free port in south eastern Sweden. It was here he learnt his trade as a sail maker. He had not seen military action though Sweden remained on high alert of Russia who had taken Finland from Sweden in 1809 and was showing interest in Finnmarken, an area at the top of Norway. There was also an emerging threat from Prussia and a joint Swedish-Norwegian task force had been offered to Denmark to fight in the first Danish-Prussian war in 1848 but it did not take part.

Anders' last ship was the *HMS Valkyrian*, built in 1852 at the Karlskrona shipyard. The steam corvette was built of wood and had three masts and twenty-four guns. When Anders left the navy, he used his money to purchase some land at Toftings. On it stood a small two storey house with living area downstairs and bedrooms upstairs. The house was built of local timber and like all those around it was red in colour, a paint made from water, flour, linseed oil and the tailings from local copper mines.

Because his farm was small, basically a residence with vegetable garden, a few cows and some poultry, Carl's three sons, Anders Gustaf (born 1861), Jan Erik (born 1866) and Carl August (born 1871), all became seamen. Each brother left home in their late teens, Anders eventually settling in Australia in 1883, Carl shipwrecked and remaining in Australia in 1897, and Jan who visited his brothers on an American ship in Sydney in 1920 but was never heard from again, presumed lost at sea.

Of their four daughters, the eldest, Maria Kristina, born in Vaddo in 1860, never married. She left home in her teens to work as a housekeeper for a pastor in Harg Parish but when her father died in 1901 she had returned to Massum, Vaddo to look after her mother who died in 1908. She remained in the family home till her death in 1930.

Johanna Kristina was born in Vaddo in 1863 and had married a local farmer from Soberdy and they had seven children. Margareta Matida was born in 1867. She had never been a healthy child and died aged twenty. Emma Josefina (born Vaddo, 1875) had left home for the city of Uppsala to become a primary school teacher and took a teaching position in Ostervala, Vastmanland. It is here she met and married a local famer Gustaf Andersson, and they had eleven children.

After being at sea for five years on various ships, Anders arrived in Sydney in 1883 on the ship the *Ellora*. As a crew member, a coal lumper, he had been ordered not to mix with the passengers but one young Scottish girl, Jane Brown, had caught his eye. Their meetings were brief, hampered by Anders' broken English and her broad accent that made him smile. Jane was bound for Sydney to live with her uncle Alex Dougan at Unwins Bridge Road, St Peters. Her father, Robert Brown a railway foreman in Glasgow, Scotland had recently died. She was travelling with her younger sister Ellen and brother James. The three of them had been educated by their father and could read and write.

Anders was due to sail on the next leg of the ship's voyage but chose to leave the ship. Though he would have very much liked to follow her, he had nothing to offer and their contact had been as friends, nothing else. He spent a few days looking for work on the docks but nothing came. He did meet people, other men looking for work, one of whom was heading west to the Blue Mountains hoping to gain work in the mines. In 1881, John Britty North had built a railway siding at Katoomba to access the kerosene shale layer. North had purchased land and mining rights in the area. He had then built a cable haulage track down to the mines at the base of the cliffs and had horse drawn trams to connect the mining sites.

Anders left his shared room boarding house in Sydney's Rocks opting to walk to the train station. He could have taken a steam tram that ran up Elizabeth Street but he considered that an unnecessary expense. It was further than he expected as the station was situated on Cleveland Street in a place called Redfern. The brick and stone building was impressive and he could see it had been built as a through station to allow the development of future tracks further into the city centre. Anders counted thirteen platforms, an unlucky number, he thought. The roads outside were dirt and there were horse drawn wagons carting an array of goods. As he had an hour to spare before his train was due to leave, he looked at the pictures of the original station that were labelled 1855. The attached cards indicated that the train ran from Redfern to a place called Parramatta. The original station looked like a temporary tin shed with a single thirty metre long wooden platform. There were also pictures of the horse drawn trams that had travelled since 1861 from the docks at Circular Quay to the Redfern Station till being replaced in 1879.

Anders found the steam train trip fascinating. The train stopped at Penrith to have a second locomotive attached for the climb up the steep grade of the mountains. The station was an important railway centre where locomotives and crews were changed and passengers took refreshment. Crossing a relatively wide river, the train entered a zig-zag arrangement to climb the first incline. He peered down the steep drop offs to sandstone lined sheer valleys, yet there were also masses of blue green trees with twisted white grey trunks. The seven-span sandstone viaduct (the Knapsack Viaduct) was amazing. The single line included many small stations, some with passing loops, and there were some tunnels that caused the thick, sooty smoke of the engine to swirl through the open windows onto unsuspecting passengers.

It was late in the afternoon when the train reached his destination, a timber platform the guard called The Crushers. Anders was confused; he was travelling to Katoomba so questioned the unusual name. The guard informed him that indeed the station was now called Katoomba but the locals used its original name, a name related to the sandstone quarry developed just north of the line producing ballast for the construction and maintenance of the line. The Crushers had become the stopping place for trains with quarrymen, equipment and wagons for transporting the ballast.

Anders asked at the platform for directions to the office of the Katoomba Coal and Township Land Co. Limited. As he walked from the platform he noticed the scaffold that surrounded a large construction on what appeared to be the highest point in town. Not completely sure he would like mining, he decided to try his luck at the building site. He had helped his father build a timber barn and sheds back in Sweden so felt he had some basic skills. A notice tacked to a post informed him the building was called The Western Star Hotel being built by F Drewett, a builder with a Lithgow address. From what had been constructed so far it was a large Victorian style building and they had already started to put wrought iron lacework in front. Sadly the site boss indicated they had a full crew so Anders headed down the steep main street towards the mine's office. Not in his wildest dreams would he have imagined that forty years later he, his brother and their families would be spending summer holidays at what was to become The Carrington Hotel.

When Anders arrived at the mine offices he discovered that the mining was mainly done by small Welsh miners using pit ponies. At over six feet Anders, was totally unsuitable for the task. His size and strength, however, were ideal for the lumping and loading of the ore at North Siding. As his work was based on the flat plateau above the cliffs and escarpment that the ore was hauled from, Anders found a room to share in South Katoomba. A series of weatherboard houses had been specifically erected for the purpose. His co-workers, mostly Scandinavian, were welcoming but on weekends at the Centennial Hotel there were many altercations especially with the loud and drunk Welsh and Irish miners. Twice he witnessed stabbings but as there was no court of Petty Sessions or lockup in Katoomba the offenders were dragged away and conveyed by rail to the lockup in Penrith, a larger settlement on the eastern edge of the mountains, on the bank of the Nepean River.

Though the work was physically demanding the wages were good and mechanisation had simplified the process. The company had hired Norman Selfe to design and build a track, called the Incline, through a natural fissure in the rock face. The Incline had an engine at the top and the base ending at the level of the Katoomba ore stream. In 1882 the company had also built a dual two foot gauge tramway from the top of the Incline to the rail siding. This replaced the original bullock drays that had carted the ore along Engine Road.

During the three years Anders spent working for the mining company he had reason to make several visits to the mine sites in the valley. At the foot of Nellie's Glen existed a sizeable mining settlement with a large hotel, butcher's shop, bakery and public hall. The quality of life here seemed similar to his own but at the Ruined Castle settlement which was predominantly made up of quarters for single men, buildings were rough huts of bush timber, bark and flattened kerosene tins. He was glad he had not been located here; the men looked dirty and impoverished.

While he was in the mountains Anders noticed an increase in what he considered the privileged classes. They stayed in gracious comfort, some comparing it to an Indian hillside resort. They came for the natural beauty, cool walks in shaded glens. By the end of the nineteenth century, economic and social changes had led to the growth of a more mobile middle class. They arrived by train and car, opting to stay at less palatial accommodation like the George Biles' hotel, which later changed its name to the Hotel Gearin, on the main road west to Mount Victoria.

In late 1886 at the age of twenty-four, he returned to Sydney again, making his way to the docks in search of work. He was surprised but delighted to find Jane Brown was still unattached and pleased when her uncle approved of him asking her to join him for a picnic in the Botanic Gardens that had been founded in 1816 by the then colonial governor Lachlan Macquarie. Though Anders was Lutheran, he and Jane were married in December 1886 by the Presbyterian minister at the Manse, 17 Wellington Street, Newtown. Anders had become naturalised and in doing so, like many other Europeans, anglicised his name to Andrew Carlsson. Anders moved from his rented room in Kent Street, Millers Point to a rented house in Brown Street, St Peters.

Anders had obtained work in the port as a coal lumper. In the early twentieth century coal lumpers had a substantial presence on the Sydney waterfront, because coal was essential for a steam-driven economy. The Sydney Coal Lumpers' Union didn't consider themselves part of Sydney's wharf labourers and their union. Unlike wharf labourers, who shifted all manner of cargoes between ship and shore, coal lumpers worked exclusively on coal with most of the work taking place out "in the stream" as they put it, on Sydney Harbour, some distance from the wharves. Their main task was to move the coal from colliers or hulks that brought it to Sydney into other vessels. There were five categories of coal lumping work. The shovelers, winch drivers and planksmen worked on the collier or hulk that was carrying and discharging the coal, and the carriers and trimmers worked on the ship that was receiving the coal or being "coaled".

Anders had worked in all these capacities, willing to take whatever work was available. His least favourite role was as a shoveler, work that was extraordinarily arduous. A shoveler had to take about sixteen pounds (7.2 kilograms) of coal in his shovel for each lift to fill a cane basket. The extreme nature of shovelling was intensified by having to work on the uneven surface of loose coal and additionally, since there was no cessation once the movement of coal began, Anders would become unable to straighten his back. After two hours he couldn't stand any more.

Coal lumpers made up a large proportion of the population living around Sydney industrial waterfront, particularly in Millers Point and The Rocks. Though made up of many nationalities they had their own closed community. Anders, like all coal lumpers, was employed casually and theoretically was able to decline jobs, however, he did the very long shifts because it looked good to the stevedore who allocated the work, and thus helped him to retain access to the work in a highly competitive environment. Although some jobs finished after a fourteen-hour stretch, Anders might then take on another job, if he could get it, because he might not get any more work that week. He was very compliant, prepared to put up with bad conditions, having quickly learnt that those least favoured usually got the worst and hardest work. On the positive side, coal lumpers were the highest paid casual labour in Sydney and if you were prepared to do the long hours the rewards were high. The job, however, did have a high level of danger and disease. Coal lumpers suffered many generalised health problems: bad backs, rheumatics, bad knees, varicose veins, ruptures, broken ribs and conditions related to working in the wet. Billy Hughes, who later became prime minister of Australia, was president of the Sydney Coal Lumpers' Union in 1905, and also its advocate. He said coal lumping affected hearts and lungs and argued that only the very strong remained in the work and coal lumpers aged forty-five or fifty were simply "the strongest who have survived", by natural selection.

By the time of the 1890 Australian maritime dispute, Anders had obtained the position of overseer on the wharves and was a strong supporter of the union movement. The Coal Lumpers' Union was registered under the New South Wales Trade Union Act of 1881. Though the strikes had started in the coal mines of the Hunter Valley they quickly spread to the wharves. Armed troops were deployed to support the police in Sydney, Melbourne, Newcastle and a number of other ports. The violence escalated against non-union labour and the property of companies operating shipping, mines, the wharves and ports. A shortage of money to sustain the strike and a plentiful supply of strike breakers eventually defeated the unions who returned to work but wage cuts of up to thirty per cent were introduced by the employers.

After the birth of their first child, Emma Wilhelmina in 1887, Anders moved his young family to 52 Kent Street, Millers Point. Built in the 1860s, this two storey Victorian terrace house had two bedrooms and featured a cantilevered balcony over the footpath, a corrugated iron veranda and attic room. The house was of painted rendered masonry, corrugated galvanised iron roof and iron lace balustrading. The small rear yard backed onto a sheer cliff, the Sydney Observatory building on top. Constant water from springs dripped down the cliff face and into their yard.

During the long economic boom from the 1860s until the depression of the 1890s, Millers Point prospered. The exuberant wool trade supported specialised firms and ships. The legendary clippers that raced to catch the first of the wool sales in England returned with passengers and goods, and by 1861 there were six large bonded warehouses in Millers Point, as well as about 400 houses and numerous pubs. The Holy Trinity Church was remodelled by Edmund Blacket and completed in 1878. This was the approved place of worship for the military establishment, while locals were more likely to attend St Patrick's Catholic Church on Church Hill. As the waterfront and its associated buildings expanded, and even as some new housing was constructed, the number of houses began to shrink and residential amenities declined.

In 1891 the family moved to 14 Merriman Street, The Rocks. This was a sandstone cottage built for the inner harbour master around 1850. On the water's edge, Anders was only a few minutes' walk to work.

Jane sadly died in childbirth in 1906. She was buried with her baby daughter, Emma Wilhelmina who had been born in 1887 but died in 1888. Emma, who was eighteen months old, had been playing with some baby ducks in a tub at their home at 52 Kent Street, Millers Point when she drowned. As Jane was seven months pregnant in 1888 they gave their second child the same name, Emma Wilhelmina. With Jane's death, the second Emma, now eighteen years of age, became mother to her four sisters and brothers, Robert aged sixteen, Mary, eleven, Ellen, nine and Gladys, two. The family moved to live with their relatives at 32 Unwins Bridge Road, St Peters.

Anders worked as an overseer for the next fifteen years, but when the children were all of working age, he moved to what the family would call a shack on Marine Parade, Watsons Bay. A solitary retirement with his colourful rowing boat used for fishing most days.

Emma, in 1909, married Karl Herman Bogran who anglicised his surname to Peterson, the name his brother had chosen when he had immigrated to Sydney earlier. Karl had arrived in Australia from Africa in 1901 as a member of the crew on the *S.S. Kassla*. He had come to Australia to join his brother, John Peterson, who lived at Alma Cottage, Percival Street, Leichhardt. John worked as a labourer on the wharves and Karl obtained a position as a coal lumper. It was Anders who invited the young Swede, originally from Gotland, home to meet his daughter.

Chapter 11

Carl Carlsson was the sixth child of Carl Andersson's children, born in Massum, May 1871. Their family had for many generations been crofters in the Toftinge area, 80 kilometres north-east of Stockholm in the Vaddo Parish. Crofters were tenant farmers who paid for their tenancy with work instead of cash. In the 1860s there were about 100,000 crofts in Sweden. As Kronobonder, tenant farmers, they lived on Crown land. The Kronobonder tenancies were normally for six years at a time. In the 1680s the Kronobonder had been given inheritable right of possession to land they used. This right could be revoked by the Crown.

The area was once called Roslagen, the name of the coastal area of Uppland province of Sweden, which also constitutes the northern part of the Stockholm archipelago. The name came from rodslag, which is an old coastal word for a rowing crew of warrior oarsmen. For Carl, his ancestors and descendants, this was where their Viking heritage came from, their ocean in the blood. A person from Roslagen is called a Rospigg, meaning inhabitant of Ros. The people of Ros also gave their name to the Rus peoples who became the countries of Russia and Belarus.

Carl's father was the fourth of four boys, Erik, Ulf, Olof and Anders. As with tradition he had been baptised the day after his birth. As the eldest two boys worked on the farm with their father, Anders, at the age of seventeen, had joined the Swedish Navy. This had been a family tradition as through the generations many of the younger sons would seek their own lifestyle, and perhaps greater freedom and sense of identity by joining the Navy. In some cases this had also resulted in a change of name as the Swedish Navy used a position title as the person's name. An example from Carl's family was Erik Ersson born 1781, who was a second son. When he joined the navy in 1798 he was given the surname Udd. The name Udd was attached to position seventy-six in a particular company, Roslags Norra Second Company. Erik Udd replaced Olof Udd who held position 76 until he drowned while on duty in 1798. Erik was to remain in the military till his older brother, who managed the family farm, died. On leaving the navy Udd could no longer keep the designation 76 name so selected the surname Hellman. Another ancestor, Nils Nohn, was also in the navy but during a naval battle between Sweden and Russia in 1789 he had been killed.

The military system in Sweden in the early nineteenth century was such that each parish was divided into sections or areas called Rotar. It was the responsibility of each Rotar to provide either one soldier or sailor for the military machine, each year. Nobility was exempt, as were the hired labourers on their land. It was the Kronobonder who this rule applied to. The main farmer in each Rotar throughout Sweden saw to it that each military position was filled. The farmers of each Rotar paid the soldier or sailor in kind, grain, potatoes, a pig etc, as well as a house to live in and a plot of ground to till.

Carl's ancestors, like most of Sweden, were Lutherans. The split between the Lutherans and the Roman Catholics was made public and clear with the 1521 Edict of Worms. The edicts by Emperor Charles V of the Holy Roman Empire, condemned Luther and officially banned citizens of the Holy Roman Empire from defending or propagating Luther's ideas, subjecting advocates of Lutheranism to forfeiture of all property. As a result, King Gustav I Vasa instigated the Church of Sweden in 1536 during his reign as King of Sweden. This act separated the Church from the Roman Catholic Church and its canon law. Lutheranism spread through all of Scandinavia during the sixteenth century, as the monarch of Denmark-Norway (also ruling Iceland and the Faroe Islands) and the monarch of Sweden (also ruling Finland) adopted Lutheranism.

To Carl the difference was cutting out the middleman, the formal hierarchy of the Catholic Church with its power and privileges. What made the Lutheran Church distinct from the rest of the Christian community was its approach towards God's grace and salvation. Lutherans believe that humans are saved from sins by God's grace alone (Sola Gratia), through faith alone (Sola Fide). They do not require the intervention of priests to seek God's grace or forgiveness.

Though he was strong in his faith there were some Church regulations he questioned. One example was the belief that after the birth of each child the mother had to again be re-admitted into the fellowship of the parish church. The Swedish State Church excluded women for a set period after they gave birth as they were considered unclean. The mother and father also could not be present at the baptism, so the newborn baby was entrusted to relatives or a close friend in the parish.

Carl started school when he was seven and continued his education till fourteen which was the legal age of leaving. The 1842 Schools Act was introduced to ensure that there would be at least one school per Socken (parish). These had to be permanent schools with a graduated teacher. However, though the Act made schools compulsory, schooling was not, thus many parents chose not to allow their children to attend as they had an essential role working on the farms, herding, helping in the home and caring for siblings.

There would be no division of pupil by age; all ages and levels in the same room. Young children initially learnt to write in wet sand kept in the classroom then to use chalk on slate boards. The teacher had to be paid fifty-three riksdaler banco, eight barrels of grain (at least half of which had to be rye), a decent house to live in, necessary fuel, fodder for a cow and a land plot, if possible. Because these wages were comparatively poor, many teachers had secondary occupations. This was assisted by the fact that rural schools were often closed between four to six months a year, at least two months during the cold dark winter and two months during the summer harvest time. Teachers were required to have complete mastery of reading and writing skills, a full knowledge of catechism, biblical history, natural history and arithmetic. An average week for a student at a teachers' college was thirty-eight hours, of which fourteen hours were for prayer and Bible studies, five hours on the Swedish language, four hours on singing instruction, three hours on geography/history and two hours on arithmetic. Until 1853, only men were allowed to be teachers. It was not till 1861 that school inspectors were appointed to ensure correct education was occurring and Normalplaner (school standards) were introduced in 1878.

Being in a rural community, Carl's school could only afford a part-time teacher and his class had over fifty pupils. The school was held in the church hall and was under the control of a local municipality school board with the vicar as chairman. These were called Folkskolan or The People's School. Carl's school was also an ambulatory school, meaning that it travelled between villages, functioning on certain days of the week in certain locations. He, like many of his friends, often missed school as chores around the farm took precedence. By the time Carl commenced schooling, his elder brother Anders had left home to become a seaman and Jan was eleven and though still at school, was large and powerful for his age, accepting work as a farm labourer or herder when work was available.

Carl also lacked interest in the limited primary level curriculum. Each school day started with Christian knowledge and biblical history. This was followed by Swedish, arithmetic, history and nature studies. The one bright spot of some days had resulted from a social reform introduced through schools by King Oscar in 1880. In a spirit of national patriotism, physical activity was promoted. Compulsory gymnastics was introduced, coinciding with the introduction of conscription, which gave the state a strong interest in educating children physically as well as mentally for the role of citizen soldiers. Carl loved anything outdoors; in summer he hiked and swam and fished in the abundant lakes, winter he went cross country skiing whenever he could.

There was another educational option, Laroverket, secondary grammar schools presided over by the national government. A large number of wealthy families transferred their sons to these schools when they were nine years old. These schools were divided into Latinlinjen with focus on ancient languages such as Latin, and Reallinjen which focussed on a natural science program and modern languages. Carl attended neither. His family could not afford to send him and he was happy at his local school. The learning of his national language was still seen as a major essential. Since a basic reading ability and understanding of the Bible was required to be confirmed, take communion and be married, there was certainly a focus, often filled by the local vicar as many parents lacked the skills and time to do the required home tutoring, though the country had been seen as having universal literacy by 1800.

As for his sisters, Maria (born 1860), Johanna (born 1863), Margarita (born 1867) and Emma (born 1875), the school act of 1842 had for the first time included compulsory education for girls. The first girls' school in Sweden had opened in 1768 and by the 1860s there were private girls' schools in most cities but with a middle class profile. The schools had relatively high tuition fees and the students had to pass a proficiency test to be admitted. From 1874 the girls' schools were partly funded by the government. It was not till 1900 that special girls' classes were developed and co-educational classes began.

Maria and Johanna were both home schooled. Their father, during the evenings and dark winters' days, taught his daughters to read and write, Bible texts and catechism his preferred sources. The girls were also taught basic arithmetic and during the days their mother taught the skills thought to make a good wife. The girls learnt to cook, sew and weave, they helped their mother with cleaning and when old enough tending the chooks and pigs, milking the cow and making the butter. Both worked with their brothers in the vegetable garden and each in their turn helped with the younger children. Margarita, who had been very ill with a fever as a young child, always looked pale and seemed weak. She did what she could but spent much of her time reading. The local teacher, a youngish lady, Miss Runesdotter, who had replaced the original male teacher, had become very close to Margarita, visiting her most afternoons and bringing her new books to read. Miss Runesdotter also instructed Margarita in Nusvenska, or Now Swedish, a democratisation of the language, less formal and closer to spoken Swedish. The growth of public schools had led to the development of Boksvenska, basically, book Swedish, simplified books in Nusvenka, in many ways designed for the children of the working class. This was a markedly different language to that in the Bible from which their father had taught Maria and Johanna to read. The Gustav Vasa Bible had been translated from Fornsvenska or Old Swedish in the 1540s. Though called Nysvenska or Modern Swedish, it was still a formal language with the complicated grammar of official documents and scholars.

This turned out to be good for Emma, the last of the Carlsson's children, who was eight years younger than Margarita, a loud, bright and inquisitive child. She, like her older sister, had a passion for reading. Although Emma attended the local school, Miss Runesdotter constantly challenged her, setting private work and readings. Emma basically idolised this smart and articulate women, in her own mind constantly comparing her to her strict and sullen mother and compliant sisters.

As a teenager Emma was passionate about the writing of Selma Lagerlof, especially her novels *Gosta Berling's Saga* and *Jerusalem*, the latter a story of Swedish emigrants in Jerusalem. Selma, also a teacher, had received acclaim for her children's' book, *The Wonderful Adventure of Nils*. Written at the request of the National

Teachers' Association as a geography book for children, it told the story of a boy, shrunk to the size of a thumb, who rode a goose across the country. It contained historical and geographic facts about the provinces of Sweden. Emma was delighted when Selma was awarded the Nobel Prize for Literature in 1909. It was these two women who had become her role models and catalysts for Emma to leave home for teachers' college in Uppsala.

Though wanting to become a sailor like his two brothers, Carl's father was concerned about all his sons leaving Sweden and asked him to give some time to help an uncle living in Gamla Uppsala who had no children and needed help. Out of duty Carl reluctantly agreed and put his personal aspiration on hold. The area was a rich farming district in the valley of the River Fyris but his Uncle Ulf, through a combination of ill health and disinterest, had allowed his land to return to native pastures with a few milking cows. The house, much larger than his parents', was run down, shingles from the roof missing, windowpanes broken and boarded over, gardens overgrown.

Ulf was pleased to see the fourteen-year-old who had only visited his home once as a small child. He remembered him decked out in a sailor suit, with cap and embroidered collar. Ulf had become distanced from the family as they had adopted the Lutheran religion while he held onto his pagan beliefs, his home containing large wooden statues of the gods Odin, Thor and Freyr. Odin was in armour and sacrifices would be made to him in times of war. Thor had a mace and sacrifices were made to him in times of famine or plague. Freyr, who Carl thought looked rather funny, had an immense erect penis, thus naturally sacrifices in preparation for marriage. Ulf told Carl that sadly there were very few followers of the old medieval Norse religion left, most living around Gamla Uppsala where the enormous Temple of Uppsala had once stood. Ulf called it Ubsola, saying it was in a town close to Sigtuna that was at that time on the shore of Lake Malaren, the royal and commercial centre some 250 years ago.

People had been buried in Gamla Uppsala for thousands of years and Carl had learnt at school about the hundreds of burial mounds from the Viking age. Here great leaders and royals were buried in their ships at the core of the mounds. During the days Carl did what he could to help his uncle. He was frail and his back arched. He actually had a daughter but she had left and had very little contact. He didn't mind the old man, he had very few rules thus giving Carl far more freedom than he had been allowed at home. Each evening Carl would listen to the stories of the old religion, of sacrifices, feasts and battles. Some were gruesome, of mass sacrifices, others just strange like the custom where a man would be thrown down a well. If he failed to return to the surface, the wish of the people would be fulfilled.

Over time Ulf explained that his faith was based on oral history, not having hand guides of rules like the Christians used. There had been books written on the Norse faith but they were basically a series of old poems and stories. He showed Carl his copy of the Ynglinga saga that had been written by Snorri Sturluson, an Icelandic historian, poet and politician, in Old Norse. Carl could not understand a word of the language but Ulf could both read and write this Old Scandinavian. Ulf indicated his universe was initially a void known as Ginnungagap. There appeared a giant, Ymir, and after him the gods, who lifted the Earth out of the sea. The world being made of Ymir's body. The earth from his flesh, the mountains from his bones, the sky from his skull and the sea from his blood.

Another evening he talked about his faith being polytheistic, each god and goddess, having human characteristics and emotions, flaws and talents. Out of his tunic he pulled small figurines of the gods that he carried with him for protection. Ulf could not accept the concept of one, all knowing, and supremely good god.

Ulf referred to animism and their belief in spirits called Vaettir, and other magical entities that were present in animals, nature and even man made things. Various kinds of elves and dwarfs also lived in the spirit realm. He emphasised the importance of ancestor worship, keeping in contact with the dead to ensure wellbeing of the living. These spirits having the power to give blessings and provide happiness and prosperity. If you neglected them they could haunt the living and bring bad luck. Ulf discounted fate. He believed that the Norns (female figures who determine an individual's fate) controlled fate and that we should approach each event as a battle that we should fight and confront with honour.

Death was also seen differently from what Carl had been taught. There isn't any dualism in death, no good realm, heaven or bad realm, hell, just an afterlife which Ulf called Valhalla. He talked about the dark side and used the term Rokkatru. This entails accepting the dark deities like Loki and the giants Jotnar and that darkness and chaos don't equate to evil; they are a natural part of the cycle of life so they deserve to be worshipped.

Ulf used the term shamanism, a focus on the development of the individual and their personal connection to the deities. This was one area that Carl could relate to. His Lutheranism seemed similar in some ways, the emphasis on personal connection rather than relying on the trappings and hierarchy of the old Catholic Church. As the main aim of the Norse religion was to secure the survival of local villages and communities, most feasts were tied to a particular village, others in farming areas to the phases of the moon and farming seasons. Ulf asked about Carl considering taking up the pagan beliefs; he simply replied there certainly was a lot to take in and consider.

Since his arrival his uncle had insisted that mead was the only acceptable drink. In North mythology, the Poetic Mead was a mystical beverage that whoever drinks becomes a scholar. This myth was recorded by Sorri Sturluson in his famous saga the *Skaldskaparmal*. The drink was often a poetic metaphor associated with Odin, the god of wisdom and magic. The honey wine was sweet with an alcoholic content of eighteen percent. Ulf had insisted Carl consume it each evening. From large hollow horns Ulf would propose a series of toasts. The first was always to Odin, drunk to victory and strength, the second to Njoro and Frey for abundance and peace. Next came a toast to the king and one drunk to their kinsmen, those buried in the mounds, that was called Minni or memorial toast. From the beginning Ulf had made it clear that his king toast was not to the current King Oscar II as he considered him a fake. The House of Bernadotte only came into power in 1818 with Charles XIV John of Sweden, an ex-French general of the Emperor Napoleon. He had been adopted by the elderly King Charles XIII who had no heir. To Ulf a real king had to have descended from the Vikings. Sometimes Carl would awake still at the dinner table, his head throbbing. At such a time he had been completely vulnerable, his fate in the hands of destiny.

The old man's condition continued to deteriorate; some days the pain prevented him from getting out of bed. The winter was the worst; the house was cold and no matter how much wood Carl piled onto the fire, the rooms never seemed to warm.

Ulf survived the winter but Carl found his request to sacrifice one of the cows as part of the March Spring Equinox, very hard to follow. Carl had faithfully fed and cared for the animals in the barn over the months of darkness and snow, they were good milkers, of value to the farm. He had killed animals before, hunting in the forest and the slaughtering of chooks and pigs for food, but he found the thought of killing as part of a religious festival abhorrent. When he informed Ulf of his decision the old man just stood and stared at him, not saying a word, walking out of the house.

By evening Ulf was back to normal, chatting about going into the village and meeting some old friends. Over the evening meal the toasts with mead took the same excessive form but Ulf had added extras, one to the Equinox and one to something he called berserker inspiration.

Carl awoke feeling cold and realised he was lying on the floor with a blanket over him. His conscious mind swam, trying to make sense of his nightmares, figures standing around him, chanting, and the pain. Looking down he realised his chest was covered with blood and he could see a pattern scratched into his skin, three intersecting triangles. Though it looked superficial it still hurt. He staggered to his feet and washed away the blood, concerned it was too much for the size and depth of the marks on his chest, but could see no other cuts or injuries. He dressed slowly and not finding Ulf in the house made his way to the barn. With a mixture of anger and frustration he demanded Ulf explain what had taken place. Ulf's black eyes stared at him, then an icy smile crossed his face.

'We held a binding ceremony, a mixing of your blood with ours.'

He held up his finger to show where a tip had been cut.

'The Valknut is a symbol of Odin, carving it into your body gave us the power to lay bonds on your mind, binding you to our community. The sharing of blood of all who were present has created a blood oath, you promising to stay and follow our ways.'

Reeling from the images of ghostly faces, of hands touching his body, of the humiliation he felt, Carl shoved Ulf, who fell backwards onto a stack of hay. He stood wondering what he should do and as he did felt the force of the old man's cane hit his neck, then a second blow to the back of his head knocking him to the ground. Ulf stood over him, still brandishing his cane in a menacing way, yelling about breaking the sacred oath, the wrath of Odin, calling him ungrateful, snarling that he had considered giving him the farm but now wanted him gone.

The latter request he had no trouble with. He scrambled to his feet, dodging more attempted blows, returning to the house and gathered his few possessions. He walked to the village where he knew the daughter lived informing her what had happened, showing her the cuts on his chest, telling her to find another victim to help her father. The women seemed shocked but he felt it was related to the comment about inheritance more than the physical and mental state of the old man.

Rather than heading east towards his parents' home, Carl made his way south to the docks of Stockholm to pursue a life at sea as a crew member sailing for Gotland, Copenhagen and Amsterdam in The Netherlands. As he travelled south he thought about his time with his uncle. Perhaps he had been lucky; his uncle had talked about the importance of the male in sacrifice. Now that he had refused to kill the cow, and denied the alleged oath, had that put his own life at risk? Ulf had talked openly about his belief in Blot, blood sacrifices, and shown Carl a large axe that he claimed had been used by his ancestors for such ceremonies. He had also explained the importance of Hlaut, sacrificial blood, which would be sprinkled on walls and over people as a blessing and that reddening an arm-ring with blood made sworn oaths legally binding and invoked the power of the gods to oversee the keeping of those oaths. He had used his knowledge of their oral history to reinforce his belief in the significance of Blot. The tale of King Domaldi from *Ynglinga saga* (or Kings' Saga written by Sorri Sturlunson around 1225) told of a famine. The first year they sacrificed an oxen but the crops again failed. The second year they gave human sacrifice but that was not enough for the gods to change the seasons thus the third year they sacrificed their king, reddening the altar with his blood, and the next season the rains returned. As he recounted his beliefs Carl noted a disturbing, perhaps unhinged expression would cross the old man's face.

There was also the well. When Carl had mentioned the quality of water in one of the farm's wells, Ulf had joked about being careful as skeletons were often found in wells. The Norse attributed great symbolic importance to wells. Odin had gained his wisdom from drinking at Mimir's well. In exchange he had to sacrifice one eye; what reward could Ulf gain from the sacrifice of a whole human? Mimir or Mim was another figure of Ulf's pagan beliefs. After being killed during the Aesir-Vanir War (a war between two groups of deities resulting in a single pantheon or group of gods), Odin is said to have carried around Mim's head as it recited secret knowledge and counsel to him.

The farm was miles from anywhere, he worked seven days a week and had met virtually no one. If something had happened to him who would know.

He wrote to his parents from Stockholm telling them why he had to leave, omitting the physical violation he had suffered. Though only fifteen, Carl was a tall strong youth so was able to lie about his age; thus at fifteen he had left home and would not return to see his parents or sisters again.

Chapter 12

Sydney 1900

The turn of the century found Lizzie and Charlie a very happy couple with a child, Maria Matilda. The family were renting a comfortable two storey terrace house at 59 Clarence Street, in Darling Harbour. Lizzie, as with all her future children, had Maria baptised the next day, in Maria's case, at St Patrick's Catholic Church in Harrington Street. The church had had Marist priests since 1868 but this was still a cause of slight disapproval to Lizzie in the fact that the priests were French, not Irish. Father Peter Le Rennetel had arrived in the colony in 1879 and become the parish priest in 1883. Noted for his strong emphasis on the sacrament of confession, he had become much loved by most of his Irish parishioners who often called him Father O'Rennetel.

There had been Irish priests in the colony, in fact the first was Father James Dixon who with two other priests was arrested as part of the 1798 Irish Rebellion and transported to New South Wales as a convict. He was allowed to have a first mass in 1803 but with the Castle Hill — Australia's Vinegar Hill, Rebellion of three hundred Irish convicts attempting to overthrow British rule in New South Wales in 1804, mass was banned. In 1817 Father Jeremiah Flynn arrived to minister to the Catholics but he did not have official sanction. The following year after ignoring Governor Macquarie's instructions he was arrested and deported. The colony's first official priest, Father John Terry, arrived in 1820 with the foundation stone of St Mary's Chapel laid by Governor Macquarie in 1821.

Charlie was surprised when Lizzie was hesitant to place Maria in a cradle he had carved for her. Lizzie insisted on knowing what wood it was made from. *What's the difference*, he thought, but was bluntly informed that if it was from an elder tree he had to get rid of it as the Irish believed that children should never be laid in an elderwood cradle, as faeries (evil fairy) would punch then black and blue and it would result in disaster by inviting the devil into their home. It should be from an ash tree as they have healing powers; as the tree had grown, so would the child. Charlie knew that elder trees did not grow in Australia but were common in his Scandinavia and Lizzie's United Kingdom, however, ash forests were plentiful in Victoria and Tasmania thus he assured her it was ash.

Charlie asked if there were any other trees he had to look out for. 'Yes, the birch, if one of its white hands touches your head it causes madness but if it touches your heart, it is the touch of death. There are the Apple-Tree-Men, you should always leave the last apple on the tree for him, to ensure future harvests. Actually there is also the oak tree, if you chop one down the Oakmen will be angry and the fungi that grows will be poisonous. Also the mushroom, they are used to mark out the fairy ring, the boundary of the faeries' favourite dancing places, we don't take mushrooms from a fairy ring.'

Charlie made a mental note never to plant birch trees or pick the last apple in any future gardens. Fungi he had no trouble with. He remembered his Uncle Ulf's tales of the Viking god Odin, a tall old man with flowing beard and one eye, the other given in return for wisdom. He was also called Woden, the god of war, who had been chased by devils with red flecks of foam falling from their mouths. When the foam hit the ground it turned into toadstools. Though considered a food from the gods, he had no intention of ever trying them. The other thing Charlie remembered about Woden was that the English language had used Woden's Day, identified with Wednesday.

'So are there any good things we can plant?' Charlie didn't really expect an answer but got one.

'Yes, the rowan with its red berries is very effective at keeping away bad spirits and the hazel, its nuts give you knowledge and increase fertility. Saint John's Wort is also very good at providing protection from faeries and has some good healing powers but there are also the bluebells, it's extremely dangerous, the colour provides a place for faeries to cast spells.'

Charlie had some concerns about the last two. While on his uncle's farm he had seen how dangerous St John's Wort could be if animals ate too much of it, but bluebells, that was something he was going to have to work on. He loved the bluebell undergrowth throughout Sweden and had planned to have beds of the flower in his own gardens. Yes, that was something he would slowly convince Lizzie was not a real problem.

The Carlssons, like most people who lived in Sydney, were experiencing a time of excitement, a carnival atmosphere as they celebrated Federation and the formation of a new nation. It had been a wonderful day with a crowd of over a quarter million people strolling through the brightly decorated streets of the city. In the afternoon they were part of the throng that flocked to Centennial Park to see the formal proclamation, by the Governor General Lord Houptoun, reading from Queen Victoria's message.

The crowd was smartly dressed all in their finest Sunday clothes. Charlie preferred the singlets and open necked shirts of his working days but on this occasion, he was pleased that he had agreed to his wife's request for a stiff starched collar and tie. From a slight rise they could see what seemed to be millions of heads in front of them and in the distance an open white pavilion. The spectacle included rows of superbly uniformed troops of many nations and a choir of thousands of children, the girls dressed in white muslin. After the ceremony there were the pealing notes of a bugle and the battalions of Australian and Imperial forces marched off in a solid mass of glittering gold braid, silver helmets glistening in the partially cloudy sky, highly polishes cuirasses, uniforms of khaki and scarlet.

'They were lucky with the weather,' Lizzie noted. Yesterday had been dark and stormy, but the sun had come out early to greet the dawn of the new nation and shine on the official procession through the city streets. Appropriately the parade had been led by a contingent of shearers who had received a grand reception from the crowd lining the street.

By St Mary's Cathedral, the vantage point that Charlie had made for early that morning, 2000 little girls fluttered their handkerchiefs for hours as the parade slowly made its way past.

Sadly, they were back in Centennial Park a few weeks later but this time for a different kind of ceremony. As they moved amongst the quiet crowds, Charlie pointed out to Lizzie how all the flags were at half-mast. Though Irish, Lizzie had respected Queen Victoria as a person and truly felt part of the common outpouring of sympathy. Charlie, less enthused, went along as he also felt a somewhat vague connected link in that Victoria's granddaughter Margaret, daughter of Arthur Duke of Connaught and Louise of Prussia, had married his king, Gustave of Sweden.

'It's amazing, this article,' Charlie said, holding a local city paper, 'says that her grandchildren are also royalty in Germany, Norway, Russia, Romania and Spain.'

Lizzie almost sniggered.

'It's the power of the ruling classes, I think the French had the right idea, Ireland would be a lot better off without them, their landlords and taxes.'

Lizzie's respect for the British Empire and the royal family only went so far.

It was a wonderful time to be living in their new country with a new life as a family. This young country was free of many of the class restrictions that caused such poverty and desperation in old Europe. Here if a man was willing to work, he could. New industries were starting up each day and the building industry boomed as wave after wave of immigrants arrived. The country, or at least some of its politicians, seemed to have adopted a "populate or perish" philosophy. This was not the last frontier but certainly a new frontier.

There was, however, one major scare for this young couple when Charlie came home with a fever. Lizzie was very concerned as she knew that her husband and the other workers had been constantly complaining about the number of rats on the wharves; he had been bitten several times. Now the unthinkable had occurred, the first reported death from bubonic plague, the Black Death. Though it was of a seaman in Adelaide, the message spread quickly as did the disease, with confirmation in Melbourne and Sydney.

Fear is a terrible thing. Lizzie couldn't tell anyone. She knew disclosure even if only a slight suspicion would result in them being immediately shunned by the community, becoming pariahs, avoided at all costs and moved to the quarantine station on North Head. She had to admit that she had done it herself, avoiding sick children, not answering the door if she felt the contact might have a detrimental effect on her loved ones.

The Australian colonial government had been concerned that the plague could arrive at any time via the shipping routes since an outbreak in Hong Kong in 1894 where 100,000 deaths had been reported that year. The world's third great bubonic plague pandemic had started in northern China in 1855. In 1896 the plague had spread to India and in early 1899 Noumea was declared a plague infected port. When it had arrived in Sydney in 1900 the response was one of fear and trepidation.

Many of the current medical practitioners and even scientists believed that the disease was spread by human contact but were also aware of the increasing evidence that it was associated with an epizootic infection in rats. Charlie had heard that the barque *Formosa*, arriving in Adelaide from New York, had cases of the plague on board. A seaman named William Eppstein had jumped ship and had since died. The first victim in Sydney was on the 19th of January 1900, Arthur Paine, a thirty-three-year-old delivery man whose work took him to the Central Wharf where the ship carrying infected rats would have docked. Arthur had lived at 10 Ferry Lane in The Rocks, close to them and other family members. The diagnosis was made by Dr Sinclair Gillies, a physician at the Royal Prince Alfred Hospital. By the end of February, thirty cases had been reported.

There were to be twelve outbreaks between 1900 and 1925 as ships imported waves of infection. During this period there were 1371 cases and 535 deaths, the disease being recorded from northern Queensland to Melbourne, Adelaide and Fremantle.

In 1896 a Dr Thompson had been appointed the president of the Health Board and a Public Health Act had been passed by the colonial government in 1897. This allowed the government power over disease control. The colonial and city governments had been proactive implementing a three-phase approach to the disease. They would transport infected individuals and anyone they may have had contact with to the quarantine station at North Head for ten days and in the first nine months of 1900, 1759 people were quarantined with 263 confirmed cases. The second phase was to consist of intensive cleaning of infected neighbourhoods. The newly formed Plague Department used lime, carbolic water and lime chlorine to disinfect houses and all waste. However, in some cases houses and sections of the dock areas were demolished and burnt. The third phase began in March with the council organising teams to exterminate the rat population. The government paid two pence per rat delivered to an incinerator on Bathurst Street. The government also provided poison to individuals as a protection strategy. Eventually nearly 110,000 rats were killed.

Lizzie and Charlie had both skimmed the eight-page pamphlet that had been issued by the NSW Department of Public Health entitled *Prevention of Plague: Instructions to Householders*. Like most they were concerned about the statements such as, "Plague is present in Sydney. It had been introduced by diseased rats, and there is great danger of it spreading" and "Plague is a fever: like other fevers, it is aided in its attacks by filthy surroundings". The pamphlet also called on families to dob in their neighbours: "Every ratepayer should make a point, of reporting every nuisance which he observes in his district". The community was also instructed, "All makeshift buildings and sheds in bad repair must be pulled down and removed from the premises". Fear related to this led local residents in Millers Point and the Rocks to burn and demolish areas considered as infected, including their own homes.

Lizzie told her family that she and Charlie had to go away on urgent family business, asking a cousin who lived only a short distance from their home to look after their daughter. Though they thought this very strange as Lizzie was terribly overprotective of her child, never letting her out of her sight, they agreed. Lizzie then locked herself away from the world, hoping that her daughter would be spared the possible contamination. She constantly sponged her semi-conscious husband to try and lower his temperature but was completely unaware of how you would treat the plague and unwilling to ask. She kept him in a dark place with blankets over the windows as she was sure there was something to do with light and effect on vision. She also wanted to ensure that no one would suspect they were home. She checked regularly for a rash or sores or even blisters as again she felt they would be symptoms. There were none.

Days passed without change but after three days of not eating he seemed weaker, and the periods of unconsciousness seemed longer. Yet there were no other visible signs; she felt a little more optimistic. Surely if it was the plague something more dramatic would have appeared. She was determined to maintain her vigil, only leaving his side to get basins of cool fresh water with which to bath him. Having not slept or eaten for the same period, fatigue finally took its toll with her collapsing in the middle of the slate hallway between the kitchen and front bedroom.

When she awoke it was dark, and waves of panic poured over her. Her arm ached from where she had fallen, her wrist swollen, perhaps a break. She struggled down the dark hall bursting into the silent front room. Stillness! She grabbed Charlie and shook him, at first a gentle shake then one that made his head rebound back and forth; she was herself shaking but emotionally, her arm now throbbed. Her head spinning she again collapsed at the sense of losing her soul mate and protector.

She awoke after some unknown period and instinctively burst into a stream of tears. Still in excruciating pain she reached out to touch his still white body for a final time.

Warmth, his skin, there was warmth, not the cold feel of death she had expected. She could still hear no breath; see no movement in his naked chest, but warmth.

With all conscious thought of public interest or condemnation gone, she ran from the house to seek help.

'It's just some type of influenza,' were the consoling words of the doctor that she had finally aroused out of a deep sleep by her almost lunatic like screaming at the locked front door of his home. 'He's very weak but his fever has broken, we need to get him into hospital, and I will need to take a look at your arm while we are there.'

Just influenza, Lizzie felt his off-handed comment to be a complete understatement as the flu itself could have been a death sentence and Charlie had developed a severe case with protracted recovery time.

Lizzie's hesitation and fear of humiliation had almost cost the ultimate price. She felt crushed by the weight of it all.

For his fellow workers and the community in general, Black Death was still a real issue and it hit closer to home with people he knew contracting this almost assured death sentence. Though some made fun of it calling them the "Pied Pipers of Pyrmont", Charlie was pleased when the Sydney City Council hired rat catching teams and distributed handbills all around the docks and throughout the city about the dangers of leaving rubbish, especially food scraps in streets or stacked behind buildings. It was a timely warning for a people who had grown a little too complacent about what were acceptable living conditions for its poorer citizens. Great relief was felt in September when the city was declared free of plague and the yellow flag that had been flown at the quarantine station was taken down.

Charlie recovered slowly and found being anything other than fully occupied exceedingly difficult. Lizzie smothered him, not letting him do anything or go anywhere. If she had her way, he would be in a wheelchair wrapped in a blanket and on a diet of soft semi food. He didn't feel like reading, except for specific interesting parts of the paper, the shipping news and world events, but during his convalescence he would go through the whole paper; there was not much else to do. As he did, he started to develop a newfound interest in the political situation of the new federal system.

The first elections of the new Federation were to be held on the 29th of March and Charlie, and with many of his colleagues from the docks, he marched and rallied in support of the Free Traders. Though weakened, often short of breath, completely against his wife's wishes, and lying to her about where they were going, both he and his brother had attended a large demonstration in Moore Street held by the Protectionists. They were going to let that mob know what they thought and how ridiculous their policies were but any intention they may have had to call out or disrupt was stopped by the incredibly supportive and vocal crowds.

This was the first time he had become aware of the resentment that was growing within his new land. Being born overseas, he and most of his friends were staunch supporters of free trade and very opposed to the idea of protection which many had attached to a call for a "White Australia". He was white but not in the context that they were referring to. Their white was a British white. It was also the first time that he clashed with his in-laws. For some reason, the Catholic Church and thus most of its followers, were strongly Protectionist. He could not see why Lizzie's family just blindly accepted what they were told. Surely, they had experienced enough British bullying. But here they were supporting a party that wanted to expand English colonial control by locking out supposed undesirable people and products.

There was violence at one rally he attended, a group of Protectionists brandishing placards yelled and jeered at the Free Trade speakers then a few of the more radical group smashed the beer bottles they were carrying and used them as weapons. Those police present just stood and watched, 'Showing their true colours,' was how Charlie described it to his brother. Charlie did not go back after that meeting; he was not afraid, just disgusted. In addition, he now had two young children and his wife was expecting their third, thus she needed him at home.

This was the first time Charlie had felt politically aroused yet at the same time experiencing a sense of frustration by what he could see as copious amounts of rhetoric and emotion and little real political action.

Despite this growing local nationalistic interest Charlie remained a true Swede and scanned papers for any news from his homeland. He was delighted in December to read that the King of Sweden had presented a new award that was to be named the "Nobel Prize". These laureates would be presented in the fields of literature, chemistry, physics, peace and medicine. The awards, funded by a legacy from the late Swedish chemist Alfred Nobel, would be "annually made to those who during the preceding year, shall have conferred the greatest benefit to mankind". Charlie had to laugh; he remembered that Nobel had been referred to as "the mad scientist" and was famous for inventing dynamite. When he raised the issue with nationalistic pride, especially in discussions with his non-Swedish friends, this fact which he avoided verbalising, crossed his mind.

'Perhaps there is irony in some of his money, from such a destructive invention, being used for good.'

The dawn of the new decade and century had been an exciting year for the Carlssons, a rush of national pride both in Charlie's adopted country and for his homeland, a chance to get involved with a new group of men and the best, the expectation of their next child.

Chapter 13

The eldest of the Carlsson children, Maria, had been born in 1899. An active and happy child her infant years were overshadowed with Lizzie's sadness at the loss of their second child, Martina in 1902, then her preoccupation with the new baby, Carl born the same year. She remembered lots of visiting to other family members' homes, all of whom lived only a few houses or streets away. Many of the narrow streets of Millers Point had been cleared or redeveloped after the plague so there was less overcrowding, but she was never allowed outside alone. Even when she started school at St Bridget's in Kent Street her mother would walk her, with baby Carl in a pram, to school then collect her in the afternoon. She was often in bed when her father came home; he worked such long hours and was covered with soot, Lizzie forcing him to wash in the tubs in the back yard laundry before being allowed into the house to change for supper.

By the time her brother Francis and sister Irene were born, Maria felt more like her mother's servant than a child. She was not allowed to visit school friends' homes and family gatherings were her only social contact. As she was quiet and compliant her teachers, Sister of Mercy nuns, treated her well. She was dependable so often was asked to help the younger girls with their writing and to organise and supervise their games. Jump rope seemed to be the favourite physical activity as the playground was small with a firm surface and equipment was limited. Maria would organise games of Blind Man's Bluff and Grandmother's Footsteps, a game where the children had to move then stop statue like. On wet days she would hold a game of Hunt the Thimble where she would hide a thimble in the classroom and the girls would hunt for it. Thimbles the school had, as they were also used when the girls did sewing, seen as an important part of the girl's education.

Maria stopped going to school when she turned fourteen, to become Lizzie's full time home help. With the birth of Esma in 1915, there was a house full of needy younger siblings. Maria had become another mother to Lizzie's youngest, Margaret born 1919 and Harold, who they all called Harry, born 1920. She was herself an adult when they were born. To them she seemed so tall and was part of a set, a boy often there, a particular boy named Bill O'Rourke. He came from another local Irish Catholic family, had a job with good prospects, regularly attended mass at the local church, thus Lizzie had approved. For the younger children, the fact he had an old car his father had given him, and on hot summer days would take them to the beach at Bondi, was enough.

It was Maria's wedding at St Francis Catholic Church in 1927 that was one of Margaret's most vivid childhood memories. Margaret was nine and was in her fourth year of school. She loved the pretty flower girl dress that she had worn and the smell of fresh flowers in her hair. Her sister, Esma, aged twelve, had also been a flower girl and Irene, aged sixteen, was one of the two bridesmaids who had worn knee length pink dresses with scooped hems and large brimmed hats that were also in pink. She could vividly visualise the hall at the rear of the church with dancing and music, the noise, never had she heard so much noise. This memory, a happier time, was captured as with so many others in heavy picture frames that hung in the Carlssons' sitting room. There was another memory of that day, less clear but that lingered in her mind for many years. She had been woken from a deep sleep by loud banging on the front door, someone screaming, her parents running followed by muffled voices then silence, this process being repeated only minutes after the first.

It would be many years before this puzzle would be solved and even then, only as part of an awkward conversation where her mother had attempted to explain the facts of life. This was something that she had not done with her eldest daughter, thus Maria had left her wedding with a sexual knowledge consisting solely of seeing her baby brother in the bath, so she knew he was physically different. Her beliefs and values were based on the nun's comments at school and church, haranguing her on the virtues of marriage and evils of sex. When Bill undressed, fully aroused, he moved to the bed where she lay; lifting her nightie he attempted to lay on top of her. She had never seen an adult male naked and the site of his erection had shocked her; she screamed and pushed him away. Bill, frustrated, became more physical but Maria, now hitting and kicking like a wild animal, grabbed her robe and ran. Her home and perceived safety was only a few blocks from the small hotel where they were spending their first night. She did not notice the cold and pain in her bare feet as she ran, gripped with terror and fear.

Though Bill considered himself experienced, this consisted only of several date related encounters in the back of his car with willing girls; he did not know how to react or what to do to rectify the situation with his young bride. Bill expected immediate physical gratification; he knew nothing of romance and was enraged by Maria's reaction to him. He had been brought up in a family where comments by his father and the dominating and sometimes brutal relationship his father had with his mother taught him that marriage was getting a nice girl to have your children, look after your house and provide physical pleasure. With his father's death he had become, in his mind, as the oldest of four boys, the man of the house and head of the family and tried to act accordingly. In reality his mother had become a very strict and domineering matriarch and was intensely jealous of her sons, a factor that would affect how each of them related to females.

Through tears, Lizzie Carlsson attempted to explain to her distraught and confused daughter about the physical part of marriage. She stumbled over words duty, creating babies and God's plan. Charlie, twenty minutes later was in the kitchen of the family home, pouring a beer for his new son in law, 'First night jitters, a virgin,' words to calm and placate.

The marriage was consummated, in darkness, and though Bill was a dutiful husband and son-in-law there was a coldness and distance. Trained as a mechanic he worked hard with very long hours to earn extra money. Bill lived with his bride in the Carlssons' Leichhardt home and as he was well paid, contributed generously to the family budget. He enjoyed taking his wife and in-laws on Sunday outings to the beach and on several occasions for a drive into the Blue Mountains where, as a family, the Carlsson's had spent many holidays.

Bill was alone in Sydney as his mother and brothers had moved in late 1919 to The Entrance on the Central Coast of New South Wales. Bill had gone with her initially to find the place and planned on eventually returning when he had saved enough money to build his own small home for Maria and himself. Maria had accepted this decision but was very happy to remain for the present in the security of her parents' home. The house was large enough for the family. It had been decided that as a married woman Maria needed her own room that Bill would share when back from up north. Charlie had enclosed a section of the side veranda, so this was to become Irene, Esma and Margaret's room plus Lizzie's sewing room. Francis kept his room that also contained a bed for Carl and Harry's bed.

The commencement of 1930 brought both the impending challenges of a new decade plus joyous news that Maria was expecting a child. Lizzie felt mixed emotions about being a grandmother but was delighted for her daughter,

'Children hold marriages together, it will make your marriage happier and better, Bill should make a great father he's so good with those two terrors, Harry and Margaret.'

Maria, who had been a sickly child was unwell throughout the pregnancy. She felt constantly nauseous, her joints ached, her legs swelled, and she looked very pale with constant black rings around her eyes. Lizzie, who had never been sick for one day during her pregnancies and had her babies with a minimum of labour and pain, found it difficult relating to Maria whose personality had changed to moody and depressed. Bill was at home less and less, for him, and to be honest the whole Carlsson family, the nine months felt like an eternity.

When the day did arrive Lizzie's concerns were founded, and Maria was in labour for thirty-six hours. The ordeal had sapped whatever life was left in Maria and just over twelve months after the birth of baby Keith she quietly slipped away to "God's peace". The loss of their third daughter, following Marian in 1901, Irene in 1928 and now Maria, stabbed deeply into the emotional chasms of Lizzie and Charlie.

The external release that was afforded by Lizzie of keening and tears of sorrow was again denied to Charlie. As with all crises, he internalised his feelings, locking himself for extended periods in his haven, his workshop at the rear of the family home. He had in some ways become a walking time bomb of repression.

With the death of Maria, Bill made immediate plans to move out of the Carlsson home. He originally talked about renting a small place of his own but within a week of the funeral he decided that the best option would be to move to the Central Coast to help his mother. As Keith was too small and frail to travel, and Bill was uncertain about what awaited him up north, the baby was left with Lizzie to care for. It was never intended to become a permanent arrangement but did. Bill continued to send regular payments for the boy's care but rarely returned to Sydney to see his son.

Lizzie enrolled Keith in a boarding school, St Joseph's College, Hunters Hill, which was a Marist Brothers Roman Catholic boys school. Besides the fact that it was Catholic, Lizzie was impressed that the school could trace its origins back to the Marist brothers' school founded in Harrington Street, Church Hill, which was attached to St Patrick's Catholic Church. That had been her church, the place of family marriages, baptisms and sadly funerals. The school had been transferred in 1881 onto land selected because it was close to the then headmaster, Emilian Pontet's, Marist Fathers' Monastery and parish of Villa Maria. Through her link with the church Lizzie had spoken to the current headmaster, Brother Louis Hughes, who had been very supportive of her concerns for the boy.

Charlie had argued against the decision as he knew he would miss the boy and the money that Bill sent would not cover the fees let alone the boarding house costs and all the extras like uniforms and school excursions. Lizzie assured him that Keith would be home on weekends but that was to prove untrue as Keith loved the weekend sporting opportunities and companionship of the other boys. Though he would not say it to the family, he was also very pleased to be away from his domineering grandmother.

Charlie was also worried that though his son Francis had completed secondary school and trained as a draftsman, the others had all been encouraged to leave school as soon as possible for employment. How would they react to Lizzie's decision? There was also the fact that Charlie considered himself a member of the working class, a strong unionist, a Labour Party supporter and proud of his achievements. The whole private school concept smacked of the upper classes, of the dock and ship owners he had battled with as he toiled on the docks. He knew that Lizzie had made up her mind; as usual she would get her way. All the family had learnt that it was better to just say yes than deal with the emotional negativity of a denied Irish stubbornness.

Chapter 14

Charlie's city changes

The initial task of the new Sydney Harbour Trust (later the Maritime Services Board) was to rebuild the wharves, but after some attempts to establish other bodies to construct new housing, this task also went to the trust. By mid-1901 it was in possession of more than eight-hundred properties, including five hundred and fifty-three houses, between George Street in The Rocks and Kent Street in Millers Point and behind Darling Harbour. For the next decade this meant only a change in landlord for most people, as priority was given to waterside reconstruction and to bringing the tramlines from George Street into Millers Point. Millers Point became a huge building site, and up to 1,000 men would congregate at the corner of Argyle and Kent streets in the morning, hoping to be called up for a day's labouring. The first wharves to be rebuilt were replacements for the larger private owners, such as Dalgety's on the point, who leased them back on completion.

For the Carlssons and other Swedish immigrant families, their custom of frequently changing houses did not change. The trust did not restrict who were to be the tenants as long as they paid on time. This resulted in the extended family passing properties from one member to the next.

Charlie had to face two losses in a short period. Their tiny baby Marian only lived for a few hours after her birth. The second loss was that of his father. It took months for the message to reach him. He thought about visiting his family in Sweden, but it was not practical.

For Charlie his new land was now becoming a nation. There had been the first Federal elections in March and the next day Charles August Carlsson and his family was now part of the national census, one of 3,773,801 "Australians", Indigenous Australians excluded. In May the Parliament of Australia was opened in the Royal Exhibition Building, Melbourne.

Lizzie thought this a good time to invite her brother Martin over. He was now working as a labourer on the railway and living in Portland Street, Waterloo. Martin had been born in 1877, one of four O'Sullivan children born in Melbourne, Mary Anne in 1876, Martin in 1877 and Patrick 1879 and herself 1880. Sadly Patrick had died in 1896 aged seventeen. Martin left the family's dairy farm in Botany to work with horses. Patrick at the first opportunity followed.

It was while breaking a string of horses that Patrick was thrown, hitting his head. They were a long distance from any medical support so wrapping his head in brown paper and vinegar was about the extent of the group's medical knowledge. Martin knew using copious amounts of cider vinegar would cleanse the wound and reduce the chance of infection. The brown paper, made from old rope, canvas and other sacking would then be used as a non-adhesive dressing, a rag tied around the head to hold it in place. He died two days later. It had taken a long time for Martin to accept it was not his fault, an accident, but there was always the nagging question. What if he hadn't encouraged his brother to join him? What if he had stopped him from riding such spirited horses, after all he was a novice on horseback and seemed to show a youthful disregard for his own safety. It was Lizzie with her glass of sweet sherry who proposed a toast in memory of Patrick.

Their father John had told the boys tales of their time in Melbourne and the work he had done in the building of the Exhibition Centre. Martin spoke as if he remembered the day and sights, but at three, Lizzie was fairly certain he was retelling and most likely embellishing on some of their father's stories. Martin still after nearly twenty years considered himself a Victorian and boasted about Victoria winning the Sheffield Shield. Being cricket, Charlie knew very little about the game let alone a competition that had first been contested in 1892.

The intercolonial matches were played between the colonies of New South Wales, South Australia and Victoria. Martin explained the shield had been named after Lord Sheffield who had donated it. He started talking about one of his favourites, George Griffen for South

Australia, and used terms like right-arm off spin, all-rounder, a nine wicket innings. Charlie smiled and feigned interest, but realised that to be part of this new British land he would have to learn something about these foreign sports. Who knew, perhaps if they had sons they might want to play this cricket game. They might even ask Charlie to help them develop their skills. He would worry about that later, if he needed to.

Still not knowing a lot more about the games, Charlie was pleased to show Lizzie a newspaper article showing New South Wales had won the 1902 Sheffield Shield competition.

It was only after this 1901 dinner that Charlie began to develop a relationship with Lizzie's male siblings. He had known Mary Anne and Maggie from the boarding house, both so much like their sister Lizzie in appearance and temperament. Both had married fellow Swedes, Mary Anne, Johan Erik Kragsterman (Sandy) and Maggie, Gustave Willhelm Carlsson, so naturally he had a lot in common with them. The three used Swedish when they met; they had shared experiences as seamen; their culture and heritage was the same. All three had seen the near slavery like conditions of the blacks in Africa, been amazed by the foods and colours of the markets in Northern Africa, and wondered at the wealth and exotic nature of the Asian cities they had passed through.

The O'Sullivans were very different, not only in appearance but also age. Besides Martin who was six years younger than Charlie, he had met a younger brother Daniel who was twelve years younger than Charlie, but he had left Sydney and become a tailor in Townsville in Queensland. John, fourteen years younger than Charlie, did not marry and though he attended extended family outings such as a picnic in the Botanic Gardens, he made little attempt to socialise with the Swedes. The younger surviving brother was Francis but he was twenty-one years younger and in attitude, dress and interests was from a different generation. A handsome, fancy dressing youth, he was a similar age to Charlie's own children.

While the Swedes had experienced the world, Lizzie and her siblings had been born in this isolated British colony. A new land that when the Europeans had arrived they called Terra Nullius, unoccupied or uninhabited. The colonial development was based on the premise that European culture was superior to all others, and that the Europeans could define the world in their terms. Of course, Charlie and his friends had quickly realised that the word British had to be substituted, and even Lizzie would narrow that to English. Certainly this new land offered greater opportunities; it was not shackled to the same extent with social class and inherited land limitations; here money bought respect and influence. Though there had been tension and even limited conflict between the government and different racial groups, especially the Irish and Chinese; these seemed quickly absorbed into the expansionist movement of the era.

The fourth addition to the Swedes had been Karl Herman Peterson, who the family called Herman to avoid having three Karls. Though he was Anders' son-in-law he had been born in 1877 making him the same age as Lizzie's brother Martin. Again language, life experience and being a member of the coal community made him much closer to Charlie. The difference with Herman was his musical talent on the piano accordion. Herman had been given his father's accordion that had been built at the Allegemeine Deutsche Industrieausstellung in Munich. Herman had taken this musical instrument with him on all his voyages. A friend maker on ship and shore, it showcased his strong tenor voice and complemented his bright and happy nature. He learnt all manner of songs from traditional folk music, to sea shanties and popular modern songs. Since his marriage to Emma Wilhelmina Carlsson in 1909, Herman had provided the musical entertainment at most family gatherings.

He also found that most people liked what was being called the real Australian ballads and sound. His favourites were Banjo Patterson's *Waltzing Matilda* written 1903, *Clancy of the Overflow* from 1889, *The Man from Snowy River* from 1890, *The Man from Ironbark* from 1892, and *Mulga Bill's Bicycle* from 1896. He mastered the words and phrasing for each and as he sang or recited his accent seemed less noticeable. These ballads were especially popular when the Carlsson and O'Sullivan families gathered for regular family picnics. Herman's song repertoire seemed endless, including, *The Shade of the Old Apple Tree*, *Won't You Come Home Billy Bailey*, *Put On Your Old Grey Bonnet*, *Wait till the Sun Shines Nellie*,

Yankee Doodle Boy, *Meet Me in St Louis, Louis*, *In the Good Old Summertime*, *Shine on Harvest Moon*, *Give My Regards to Broadway* and *La Donna e Mobile* which he would sing in Italian.

These picnics were a favourite family outing held either in the Domain or Botanic Gardens. Family photos showed that Lizzie and the other women of her generation still treated them as formal outings with long silk dresses, large shade hats, often with nets, and buttoned up boots. It would not be till the mid-1920s that Lizzie would venture out in a high neck blouse, calf length skirt, stockings and sensible shoes. For the men coats, ties and hats were the call of the day. The older males wore the derby or fedora though Gustave Carlson favoured his Panama hat, but the younger generation wore straw boaters. Picnics generally consisted of sandwiches and cakes wrapped in large white linen serviettes and packed in a wicker basket. On special occasions there were also cold meats, fruit, sweets and beer for the men and sweet wine for the ladies. For children, homemade lemonade was seen as a special treat.

Chapter 15

Carl August Carlsson 1902–1981

Carl was born in October 1902 He was born in the family's rented home at 7 Margaret Street, Millers Point. Like his sister, he was baptised at St Patrick's Church, Harrington Street. Their fourth child, Francis John, would be born in 1908 but at 73 Kent Street, Millers Point, the change in residence a product of Lizzie's Irish belief that having a second child born in the same home was bad luck and could lead to the child being unwell.

Carl's siblings always smiled at a photo that hung over one of the fireplace mantlepieces in the family home. An innocent, soft and gentle face beaming with importance, crowned with a white naval cap, blue band and gold lettering, Carl would have been about nineteen when the photo was taken.

The eldest of the Carlsson boys, Carl's two youngest siblings, Margaret and Harry never related to him as a member of the immediate family as he had joined the navy and was rarely at home. On the odd occasion he was, they remember being repeatedly rebuked by their mother for making noise. Carl could do no wrong in Lizzie's eyes; he was special. The fact that he never wrote to his family when he was away and that while on leave from the navy he was either out with friends, drunk or asleep, was overlooked.

Though not an academically inclined child, he had eventually developed a love of reading and his mother Lizzie would sit with him for hours helping him expand his understanding. Mark Twain's *The Adventures of Tom Sawyer* and *The Adventures of Huckleberry Finn* sat on his shelf, dog-eared and worn from constant use. To entice him Lizzie would read a page then he had to read the next paragraph; she would then read the next page. Though this caused initial frustration, and many sessions of anger and rebellion, the strategy finally worked.

To Lizzie, the books were purely words and language skills that had to be and were going to be learnt. Carl, however, associated with the characters, especially Tom Sawyer, a likable amoral rogue, self-interested but with a good sense of humour. The same with Jules Verne's *Five Weeks in a Balloon*, *Journey to the Centre of the Earth*, *Twenty Thousand Leagues under the Sea*, and *Around the World in Eighty Days*; all were read over and over, whetting his appetite for adventure and excitement. At night he would dream about great adventures, fanaticising that he was like the leading men and heroes in Robert Ballantyne's books "noted for great depth of chest, breadth of shoulders and development of muscles". He would stare at any men he met who looked like that, admiring their bodies.

His games were based on characters from the books but most of the time he would have to tell his friends about the plot and characters so they could be involved as well. Boys only; he saw girls represented in his world of books as silly weak things, irrelevant in the lives of his heroes. Men had adventures together; females, with their fainting, frailness and unsuitable clothing only got in the way.

Another frequently devoured set of readings was *Robinson Crusoe* and *The Swiss Family Robinson*. He loved the thought of fighting pirates and being cast adrift, lost on a desert island. The works of Rudyard Kipling introduced him to Mowgli's wolf pack and the achievements of Captain Courageous, enhancing his desire to experience the world. The works of William Henry Kingston also excited him with his stories of young Englishmen seeking adventure in the wilderness, coming home tougher having learnt the lifestyle of hunters and natives. Kingston's *Peter and the Whaler* and *The Three Midshipmen* greatly influenced his feelings about the future direction for his own life, about going to sea.

Carl, like his older sister, attended St Bridget's Catholic school at 14 Kent Street, Millers Point. It was on the west facing slope of Observatory Hill, a sandstone bluff which separates Sydney Cove from Darling Harbour. It had been built in 1835 as a single storey sandstone building containing a classroom and separate chapel. A partition of folding doors divided the interior in half, providing separate classrooms for the boys and girls. Pupils were initially under the care of Christian Brothers, but by the 1870s the school had been taken over by the Sisters of Mercy. Many of these were young nuns from Ireland who themselves had limited education. In the 1930s a parish priest from St Patrick's, Father Daniel Hurley, added a second storey on top of the original school.

Carl's father, like generations before him, had been a sailor but Charlie had not been supportive or encouraging of his son following in his footsteps. He knew too well the hardships and dangers.

As a young man Carl was slight of build and loved all water sports, especially swimming and sailing. He had a strong baritone voice, singing equally well angelically in the church choir or the dirtiest ditties when with football mates. As a natural entertainer he was also the life of family parties, singing, telling jokes and showing off his ability at dancing. He lacked the inhibitions of his parents and at school was considered loud and disruptive by the nuns who tried to tame his vivid imagination. This was tempered by the fact that he was particularly close to, and protected by, some of the younger priests teaching sport and music. There was even, for a short time, discussion about him joining the church himself. This idea was strongly encouraged by his mother and to an outsider it may even seem to have been her decision. Carl could remember her saying, 'It's the most noble of all professions,' and 'You have been given gifts for God's purpose.'

A son as a priest was certainly a status symbol, a physical manifestation of her family's beliefs and devotion.

At fifteen he rebelled, coming home from one of the church retreats, indicating he was not going back to school. The priesthood was out, he refused to go to mass with his mother, and though living in his parents' home he adopted a very independent lifestyle. He worked in a city clothing store until 1922 when on his eighteenth birthday he joined the Royal Australian Navy. This surprised most of his family as he was considered a bit of a dandy. His clothes were of the latest style, his thick black hair greased, meticulously shaped and there was always an aroma of sweet fragrance, too much aftershave or cologne.

After his first term in the navy Carl had moved to Western Australia and was absent from the Carlsson home until 1927. Even then he was only an infrequent visitor for about ten months, sleeping over when nothing better was offering before he left again, never to return to their Ramsey Street home.

Margaret remembered that except for her father having an occasional cigar with his brother and in-laws when they attended Saturday evening fights at a local hall or during their card evenings, Carl was the only member of his siblings who smoked. Margaret could remember the small tin of tobacco and papers he would carry, rolled into the left sleeve of T shirts and short sleeved casual shirts. She was sure he did it mainly to expose the tattoo of two anchors crossed with a ship's name below, another status symbol. This was the public one but there was another, a larger more spectacular tattoo that Francis was sure he was the only member of the family who knew about.

One day, on the way home earlier than usual from school, he had been walking along the side passage of the house and heard a loud crash from the room he was passing. Though the curtains were drawn there was a gap and he peered into the semi darkness. Two figures were wrestling. Francis recognised Carl but didn't know the other male, a youth, but both were completely undressed. It was then he noticed his brother's second body decoration. It was across his buttocks; a line of human figures also appearing to be involved in a series of wrestling positions. He had seen something like it before in a book about ancient Greeks but in those pictures the figures were decorating ceramic platters and wall tiles. He knew he couldn't tell anyone, he would get in terrible trouble for spying so he just locked it away, smiling at his little secret.

Carl, though unremarkable in many ways, did however have a special gift. He had a natural musical talent with the ability to hear a tune and then sit at a piano and play it. He could play anything and never needed or used sheet music. This would be Carl's redemption in later life. A lost soul with no apparent ambition or plans, he would make his living playing piano in bars, clubs and on cruise ships. He lived a transient life, hard drinking, too much smoking and only male friends. Carl was always surrounded by other young men, no close friends in particular and faces changed every visit. Whenever he and his friends were home they would, as her mother called it, 'Camp in the boy's room.' His brother Francis who was fourteen years younger and normally shared with Carl would be moved in with the girls, 'To give Carl and his friends privacy.' His brother and sisters had been told never to disturb Carl and his friends.

It was only in later life that a bond or at least a limited and conditional relationship developed between the siblings, this shaky alliance forged out of mutual need.

Chapter 16

1907

The coal lumpers worked for fourteen hours a day on average, in thick dust, often in only a loincloth and boots due to extreme heat. In March 1906 the Arbitration Court had set distance and weight of baskets the men had to carry, but though the employers ignored this the court took no action against employers. Employment by the Stevedore employers was basically zero hours, no guarantee of employment, but workers having to sign an agreement they would work when called by employer. In April 1907 the Stevedores Association had issued seventy summonses to members of the Coal Lumpers' Union who had not turned up for work. The situation on the wharves developed into a lockout of union members. Fortunately for the unions the Newcastle coal trimmers refused to coal up vessels normally coaled in Sydney and this weakened the employers' position. Added to this, the Wharf Labourers' Union was encouraged not to work as scab labour and media pressure worked to develop a negative attitude to the use of Chinese, Malay and Arab workers.

Charlie felt a sense of wider comradery when he attended a meeting at the Protestant Hall with fiery motivation speeches by Ben Tillett and Tom Mann, who had both led victorious London Dock strikes in 1889. The hall was packed with hundreds turned away. The following day, despite Lizzie's protestations, especially as they had a newborn, Charlie joined a crowd that paraded towards the Socialist Hall. There was another packed-out meeting for trade unionists only on Friday night, a large open air meeting in front of the Newtown Town Hall. Despite heavy rain Charlie also took part in a march of over 2000 unionists through the city streets to a rally of around 10,000 in the Domain.

Lizzie was also aware that not all gatherings had been peaceful or safe. On the 2nd May, when the Nordeutscher Lloyd steamer the *Prinz Sigismund* was at the company's wharf at Circular Quay, waiting to have coal loaded, several hundred strikers had gathered. When scab non unionists marched down with a police escort, the crowd set on them. About twenty of the non-union labour were injured in what was described as a brutal assault. A strong force of police arrived in support and six unionists were arrested. Charlie had been there, not as a striker but as one of the thousands of excited spectators watching the later stages of the disturbance.

It was a long and hard fourteen week lockout, but the workers were then able to return to work with substantial gains in pay and overtime rates and generally improved conditions. Even Lizzie felt angry when during the lockout she watched dozens of men from other unions working alongside blackleg non-unionists and heard Anders and Charlie discussing the failure of the so-called working class politicians to fight with the workers. The Carlsson family, especially its men, expressed greater anger when the New South Wales premier, Sir Charles Wade, introduced a new law that removed the right to organise indoor political meetings on Sundays and public holidays, the days when working men should be able in their own time to meet. Secretly Lizzie felt this was a good law; she held strong Catholic values and considered Sunday God's day. If the men didn't see it that way, it was at least a day when the men should spend time with their families.

There was a positive in the area of wages with Justice H.B. Higgins establishing a guaranteed minimum daily wage. The Harvest Judgement ruled that an employer was obliged to pay his employee a wage that guaranteed them a standard of living which was reasonable for a "human being in a civilised community" to live in "frugal comfort". The wage rate was set at seven shillings per day or forty-two shillings per week for an unskilled worker, regardless of the employer's capacity to pay.

In August 1908, with his six-year-old perched on his shoulders, Charlie, with thousands of other Sydney siders, lined the harbour for the arrival of the Great White Fleet. This was a popular nickname for a group of United States Navy battleships on a round-the-world tour. The American President Theodore Roosevelt sent the fleet to make friendly visits to numerous countries while displaying new

US naval power to the world. The sixteen battleships and supporting escorts had their hulls painted stark white. One goal was to deter the threat being posed by a powerful Japanese naval fleet. In Australia the visit was used to encourage support for the forming of Australia's own navy. With Federation in 1901 the Australian colonial navies had been combined to form the Commonwealth Naval Force but until 1913 Australia only had a Green Water Navy, intended for local defence. The Blue Water, a maritime force capable of operating globally, remained in the hands of the British Navy.

During the night the White Fleet lit up the harbour as each ship turned on their powerful search lights. The result was spectacular, a sky ablaze blocking out the stars.

Much to Martin O'Sullivan and Lizzie's displeasure, Charlie made it clear that he was very supportive of the decision that to settle the feud between New South Wales and Victoria the capital of his and their new country should be neutral. With Federation an agreement had been reached that a capital would be established in New South Wales so long as it was at least 100 miles from Sydney, with the seat of government to remain in Melbourne. The capital city was selected in the Yass-Canberra area in 1908 and formally named in 1913. A blueprint by American architects Walter Burley Griffin and Marion Mahony Griffin was selected after an international design contest. The entry by Elial Saarinen of Finland placed second and Professor Alf Agache of France third.

Chapter 17

1909

On 1st April 1909 Charlie penned a letter to relatives in Sweden. He had received a letter from his sister, Emma Josephina Carlsdotter, informing him his mother had died in December 1908. It was the custom in Sweden that when both parents had passed away some guardians were appointed to protect the inheritance of members of the family living overseas, for a number of years. If they could not be contacted the property would be given to a needy relative or to the local government for poor relief. Because Charlie had been corresponding with his parents and sisters, by Swedish law the property would pass equally to him and his brothers. After talking to his brother Anders, who Charlie had always referred to as Gustaf when writing to his family, they decided that as no one knew even if their brother Jan was alive he would indicate that the three brothers wished to give their parts to their sister Maria.

'She is now old and alone. If our small parts can give her a few crowns we think it will be a good help. We have sent her a letter giving her full control.'

Maria was to live in the family home till her death in 1930 when Charlie's younger sister Emma and her family moved into the family home.

Having been in his new country for over ten years, Charlie had started to take on the behaviours and patterns of his new society. He was really living in two worlds, the old of his Swedish relatives and friends and the new with the men he worked with, those he associated with related to his growing interest in unions and politics, and even his neighbours, a mixing pot of European backgrounds. Though he and Carl kicked the round ball of European football, Carl had been given for Christmas an oval shaped ball for the Australian sport of Rugby League. Charlie had read in the paper that this sport had recently had its inaugural premiership at the end of winter 1908. There had been nine Sydney based teams and one from Newcastle. Charlie considered the list and wondered if it was the Balmain or Glebe team he should call local and settled on Balmain. The reason was geographical but he also didn't like the name The Dirty Reds, the nickname of Glebe due to their maroon coloured playing jerseys. The other choices had been Eastern Suburbs, Newtown, North Sydney, South Sydney, Western Suburbs and Cumberland. South Sydney had taken the first premiership over Eastern Suburbs. The Cumberland team, The Fruit Pickers, had only lasted one season, folding after finishing last. The club had been formed the day after the first round of the premiership. At a meeting held at the Horse and Jockey

Hotel, Homebush, twenty-three players from the Western Suburbs Rugby Union Club signed up to play.

The men on the docks had talked about this, and how this Australian game was challenging the upper class, British game of rugby. Charlie knew nothing about that game either. He had read that in 1907 a New South Wales rugby union team had played the New Zealand team at the Sydney Cricket Ground and that 52,000 spectators had attended, the largest crowd to any football contest in Australia and any rugby match in the world.

Charlie found this football even more confusing when Lizzie's brothers talked about their Melbourne rules football which they also called Victorian rules. They had told him that it was totally different, a much faster and cleaner game, emphasis on kicking, not the dangerous tackling of league and rugby. They were supporters of The Demons, also called the Melbourne Football Club. It was the club their father John O'Sullivan had followed when they lived in Melbourne in the 1870s. The club, with its red and blue jerseys, had been formed in 1858 and was the world's oldest professional club in any football code. It had been formed at the request of Tom Wills, the captain of the Victorian cricket team, as a football club with its own set of rules to keep cricketers fit during winter. Initially confined to only members of the cricket club, in 1859 others were allowed to join in. While the O'Sullivans were still living in Melbourne, the club in 1877 became a founding member of the Victorian Football Association. John could not afford to go to a match or even have the money to purchase a paper but there were always discarded papers, sometimes a few days old, a bit wet or dirty, that he would read to the boys, news and sport.

On the political front Charlie was amazed when the Protectionist Party and the Free Trade Party merged to form the Fusion Party led by Alfred Deakin. The Free Trade Party had been formed in 1887 advocating the abolition of protectionism, especially tariffs on imported goods. Charlie agreed with this. Working on the waterfront he wanted as much trade, thus as many ships as possible. He saw this leading to greater employment and thus economic prosperity. However, the Protectionist Party, also formed in 1887 advocated protective tariffs, arguing it would allow Australian industry to grow, thus also proving employment.

Charlie could see the only ones gaining from this was the ship and factory owners. It had been led by Sir Edmund Barton and Alfred Deakin, who were the first and second prime ministers of Australia. The merge made no sense to Charlie and he was even more concerned when it was announced the new party was to be called the Liberal Party. Charlie had voted for the Protectionist Party but now found they were in opposition to his labour and union beliefs. He had not considered voting for the Australian Labour Party as he thought they sounded too much like socialists. He could see and was living the inequality of a capitalist society but the thought of a worker revolution, and co-operative ownership, he considered dangerous. While Charlie had been crewing on an American ship other crew had talked about the Great Railroad Strike of 1877 that had involved an estimated 100,000 workers with riots, destruction of property and violent crackdowns. He was happy in his new land and he didn't want that type of civil unrest happening.

Chapter 18

The 1920s — Happy times

Each summer the Carlsson family went on holidays. These were extended family affairs with Charlie's brother and their families joining in. On some occasions the ranks were swelled by favoured members of Lizzie's family. They alternated venues each year, a holiday home at Umina Beach, a remote beach on the Central Coast three hours north of Sydney for four weeks one year, and three weeks spent at Katoomba, the major town in the Blue Mountains, staying at the Carrington Hotel the next.

Katoomba had considerable significance to the Carlsson family as when Charlie's older brother arrived in Australia in 1885 at the age of eighteen his first employment had been in a mine in that area.

His five years in the mountains had given him a love of the peace and beauty that he had only found in this special unique portion of Australia. Thus family holidays consisted of bush walking and relaxing in this scenic wonderland filled with light and shadows, the sky of a transparent sapphire blue. The Blue Mountains had been a drawing card for many city dwellers looking for the coolness of altitude on hot summer days and being attracted by the appearance of the mountains themselves with their blue haze, an optical phenomenon called Rayleigh scattering where small particles of dust and water in the atmosphere are illuminated by sunlight reflecting the colour of the sky.

Even though the Carrington Hotel was only a very short walk from the railway when the Carlssons arrived for their biannual mountain holiday Lizzie insisted on taking the wagon that carried the luggage. The younger members of the family would run ahead while the other adults strolled along behind the carriage.

The hotel originally known as The Great Western was opened in 1882 and then purchased by Mr F Goyder, a squatter from Queensland and the first mayor of Katoomba, who immediately set about adding wings doubling its size. He had improved the facilities and standard of the hotel and changed its name to the Carrington. This had been in honour of the then governor general of New South Wales, Lord Carrington, who was a frequent guest. By 1905 it was advertised as "The largest and best known Tourist Hotel in the Southern Hemisphere". The three storey brick edifice with iron lacework on the balcony and a grand viewing platform on the roof dwarfed the little mountain settlement.

Lizzie and Charlie's first visit had been in 1899 and they had stayed at The Clarendon Private Hotel in Katoomba Street. This guesthouse was operated by a Mrs Simonson, one of Katoomba's earliest guesthouse keepers and a lady with whom Bridget felt complete synergy. Mrs Connie Simonson had been born in the Irish town of Tralee and they spent hours talking about the "home country". Her husband had been a local builder and their converted home of a stone ground floor and timber first floor and attic rooms became a source of income by renting out rooms.

The women's special bond was Irish fairy Dom, the magic domain of fairies. It was much later that Lizzie's children understood that some of the rituals their mother undertook and which they thought rather strange were actually grounded in this alternate and conflicting belief to her dogmatic Catholic core.

The children could remember years later reading their mother's private diary of the time, fascinated by an entry that described her bathing costume.

It was the prettiest I had seen in Sydney but a little daring as the full Turkish trousers finished at the knees with a band and buckle. My arms looked so white in the sleeveless black serge blouse that had a lovely sailor collar in an ivory shade. When I bought it there was an accompanying sash in the same creamy white colour of the collar, black shoes and a tiny fisherman's cap. I wore a cape over it when we walked from the hotel to the swimming venue. Even Charlie commented on how nice I looked. It felt good.

January 1899.

The children were surprised as they remembered their mother being publicly so very conservative, having commented about being horrified that some bolder girls were seen cycling.

We met a fascinating man today, Harry Peckman, a local poet and songster who has a fleet of wagonettes taking people around the local attractions. He told us about driving the Duke of Edinburgh's royal party to view the Wentworth Falls waterfall. He has met so many important people, heads of state, parliamentarians and international visitors. He was just a normal person so we chose one of his men to take us on a tour to the Jenolan caves in a sulky. We stayed two nights in the hotel, a two storey, veranda wrapped wooden building. We ate in a beautiful Silurian limestone building and were told the stone had been quarried locally. I was shocked at the cost to stay, ten shillings per adult, five shillings per child and servant. We visited two caves, the Imperial and the Lucas with their impressive limestone formations. The grand arch was amazing and next to it a very pretty blue lake, we even saw a platypus, the first time for either of us.

Through the happy years of the twenties Katoomba was a family Mecca. Even in the late twenties and early thirties when Australia was experiencing a serious economic depression, Lizzie insisted they had their time away.

This is my solace, a preferred reality, not the limitations of economy. This is the real me, here above all other places I find happiness. Change is for the young, and I like this grand lady treasure, the certainty of the old ways and cling to the past. This is my Fairy Islands, Tir Nan Og, a land of happiness, peace and plenty. There is no aging or disease for all things grow in abundance.

January 1909.

There were many changes over the time. In Katoomba, Saturday night at the pictures had become the major attraction for the Carlsson family children. The Empire and The Kings vied for patronage, the former advertising itself in 1909 as "the most up-to-date and best appointed picture theatre in the state". These provided hours of enjoyable distraction.

There was great excitement at the addition to the holiday landscape with the opening in 1911 of the Katoomba Amusement Company. It had been set up especially to supply quality indoor evening and holiday entertainment. The building was on the corner of Katoomba and Main Street and boasted a 1000 people theatre hosting plays and live theatre, a skating rink operating three times a day to the strains of a ladies' orchestra and a roof garden with glass arbour where patrons could enjoy the mountain scenery. Roller skating thus became a popular day time activity for the Carlsson children either at the Amusement Company or the other rinks in Katoomba. They, unlike many of their friends, were not allowed to skate at the hotel or in the streets. Lizzie thought this common and inappropriate.

The simple pleasures of life are being lost, swept up in modernisation. I yearn for happier times, private family times when we did things together, everyone in their own station, not fractured by increasing choices and conflicting demands.

January 1913.

When they arrived in 1913 they were greeted by the electrification of the hotel, which had its own powerhouse and the famous tapering octagonal chimney stack that dominated the town's skyline.

During the First World War, lobbying by the Temperance Movement had brought about the situation known as the "six o'clock swill" that Lizzie found disgusting and would not allow any of their extended family to be involved. She insisted that all day outings were well concluded and the children were in the safety of the hotel before the local men who had drunk as much and as fast as they could were ejected from hotels at the six o'clock closing time. From their bedroom windows they had seen many unsteady figures being marched off to the town's lockup.

Licentiousness and evil spreads even to special protected places. I worry for the world and my children. Freedom can lead to decline and loss of purity. Once doors were unlocked, free of bars, children were free to roam, safe, wrapped in this place's shawl of decency.

January 1917.

In the twenties the family, as with many holidaymakers, began bringing their new Box Brownie cameras to the mountains, the local pharmacy providing film and printing: "Developing and Printing at city prices, utmost care and promptitude".

Gramophones with large horn speakers brought the latest tunes but people would still gather around the hotel piano in the evening singing all the old classics. Evening card parties were also popular with the older Carlssons though another highlight for future trips occurred in their 1925 visit with the first ice-cream sundae being made at the Paragon café, a treat for all family members. Treasure hunts and paper trails were also popular activities for the Carlsson children, with parlour games and fancy dress parties being run by many of the hotels.

Lizzie's dairy indicated that she was not impressed with notable changes to their favourite hotel with the addition of an Art Nouveau façade. The former veranda was enclosed with Doric columns lining a tiled piazza below an undulating Italianate balcony surmounting a wall of beautifully designed stained glass. This grand entrance was approached by twelve broad semi-circular steps with ornamental white freestone balustrading.

Lovely lady, we have both lost so much. We both have exteriors that hide our past remembrances. Why couldn't people accept us as we were? Why do they expect us to change to meet their needs? I want time to stand still, the Earth to tip on its axis and spin backwards towards happier, simpler days.

January 1925.

In 1927 they stayed in the new wing that had been added, taking the hotel to a total of two-hundred bedrooms. This was the year that the Duke and Duchess of York had also been in residence.

The children especially loved the central dining room with huge columns, rich stained glass, fine chandeliers and rich furnishings. They were fascinated by the ballroom where they stood watching their parents dressed in their finery dancing the nights away and the many elegant paintings and ornaments. Lizzie's diary described the hotel as,

A beautiful woman with many facets, her face and body changing with every outing. She provides the care and welcome demanded of her status and stature. Even aging old women have their place, they uphold the traditions, they remember the important values and service that once were commonplace but now slip by unnoticed. She tries thanklessly to hold on but one by one time will strip away her jewels.

In spite of the death of Irene in 1928, in June 1930 Margaret and Harry stood with their father and hundreds of others waiting for Amy Johnson who had just become the first woman to fly solo from England to Australia. She arrived at The Carrington at one p.m. and they called out with the others 'Johnny, Johnny.' This was the last year that they would travel together as a family to The Carrington. By 1932 the dynamics of the family had changed.

On the alternate year the extended family holidayed at the beach in a house they rented at Umina. At first they caught the train to Woy Woy and then a local taxi to the home they had rented for the summer season. In later years they drove in the family car which broadened the range of activities that the family could access.

The cottage they rented was one block back from the beach, a large wooden home with two enclosed verandas that accommodated the children and four bedrooms that had adequate bedding for the adults. Usually their party consisted of Charlie, Lizzie and children, Anders, his wife Jane and their four children. There were also the add-ons and drop-ins. Several of Lizzie's sisters and their families tended to come for a few days that usually stretched into weeks. It was open house, everyone welcome, well almost, provided, of course, that they met Lizzie's standards. She had adopted the status of matriarch and though she didn't say much when you overstepped the mark, it was she who made sure you and all present were aware of it. All tended to be compliant and seemed very close.

The children, however, could remember one occasion that did cause a fairly major rift. Michael, one of Lizzie's sister's children, brought with him his current girlfriend. Margaret found her to be very pleasant and friendly but something was wrong. Her aunty and uncle were both upset, her mother was cold and indifferent and the other adults also seemed to shun and reject her. The pair left on their third day, Michael yelling at his parents and Lizzie about being bigoted and racist. She asked her father who explained that Doris was part Aboriginal and Michael's parents and most of the family did not approve of the relationship.

'He could do much better.'

This had been made worse by the fact they had openly being carrying on a sexual relationship within Lizzie's hearing. Lizzie would ignore and believe innocence unless she was confronted with what she deemed as immorality.

For the children and men, the Umina days were filled with swimming, fishing and hours of cricket but for the women preparing meals for the family, reading, handicrafts and endless rounds of what could only be called gossiping or "one-upmanship" seemed to adequately keep them amused.

These holidays also provided a break for family members from the rigid rules that were imposed on them by strict, traditional families. Many of the younger members found first love and sexual encounter on remote beaches or walks through nature's wonders. Others dabbled in the simple vices of smoking or drinking alcohol. The locals, especially those near their beach home, seemed wilder, less constrained and certainly more worldly. They were even allowed to wander around the streets after dark, and alone. This was certainly denied to the Carlsson children. For Margaret a first kiss with a boy behind the boat shed and skinny dipping with some of her female cousins was as wild as it got. Her younger brother Harry seemed to act as a social barrier, always there, but her fear of her mother's wrath was the main reason.

It didn't all go smoothly. A cousin had overstepped the boundaries getting herself pregnant to a local boy. Margaret expected it to be the end of their holidays but the boy, with a degree of encouragement from Anders and

Charlie had done the right thing. They put on a brave face but behind closed doors Lizzie in her diary wrote in a more personal format than usual, horrified.

The foolishness of youth, what a folly. Where are our tried and true standards going? I find the man to be a no hoper and lecher, mark my words I am sure Ellen isn't the first young girl he has got pregnant and I fear and regret she will not be the last. I hold fast with my strict parenting, his parents, what type of role models can they be? Mrs Watson from down the road knows them, drifters and not even married themselves, living in sin! Poor Maureen, how can she show her face in public again after what her daughter has done? The poor child born a bastard, my God, show your mercy. If any of my children did this to me I would have to disown them.

In public, however, at least on this occasion, all pretended that nothing abnormal had happened and a few months after the marriage the formal declaration of the pregnancy was made; eventual premature birth, of course.

Margaret felt sorry for Ellen, she really didn't like the boy that much. He was very handsome with sun bleached blond hair and a defined body that came from extensive exercise, but Margaret considered him dumb and unkempt. He also attempted to have sex with any girl who showed the slightest interest. This wasn't to stop after the marriage, resulting in several other young girls being placed in a similar situation but now to a married man. Barry also had no interest in working so Ellen, a girl who Margaret thought had so much promise, was destined for poverty and five additional children in a tiny house that Ellen's parents bought the couple in Woy Woy. Wisely, though they bought it for their daughter, it was registered in their names ensuring that Barry couldn't get his hands on it.

In years to come Margaret would ponder the question of genetic traits versus environment as none of Ellen's children were ever able to develop a successful or lasting relationship. A couple were bright enough, fortunately taking after their mother, but all were lazy and settled for soft options. Barry had signed up to fight in World War Two, mainly to escape the responsibilities of being a father but had been killed while fighting against the Japanese in the Philippines. Ellen's letters to Margaret after Barry's death expressed sentiments of relief rather than loss or sorrow.

Chapter 19
Irene Margaret Carlsson 1911–1928

Irene, the fourth Carlsson child, was born in 1911 at 63 Kent Street, Millers Point, a two storey terrace house, part of a three house block having stucco walls and iron roof behind a roof parapet. Built in about 1870, the house had French doors opening onto a cantilevered cast iron first floor balcony. With the house came the neighbour. Old Ma Leonard who lived at number 61 was a well-known character. She rarely moved from her chair in the open doorway or just outside on the footpath. She knew everyone and everything.

Family photographs showed Irene to be a girl of remarkable beauty. Though her mother would never talk about her after her death in 1928, Margaret and Harry, during their many long talks with their father in his backyard workshop where he made toys and repaired everything, quizzed him about her.

Often they thought they saw tears trying to form in his eyes as he told stories of Irene dancing on stage with such grace that others would stop and watch her every move. She had also been her father's helper and loved sharing his time, talking to him and listening to his stories about his life as a sailor and his family back home in Sweden. She was a bright light, full of fun, and in addition to her dancing was a good pianist. Her results at school were good and the nuns at St. Fiacres had suggested that she continue her education as far as possible. She learned the Swedish language to a point that she and father could converse, cutting out the rest of the world around them.

Irene was to become a victim of tuberculosis. Until she became too ill to function without assistance she had been very close to her younger sister Esma, sharing a room and sometimes a bed for comfort or solace. Her father would never understand or forgive God for taking his jewel from him. Reluctantly he told of the visits to their daughter in the Bodington Sanatorium at Wentworth Falls. He had shown Margaret a pamphlet about the sanatorium; it looked a bit like an advertisement for an expensive hotel. It was a specialist treatment centre built by a Dr Sinclair, built in Federation style with expansive gardens that followed the contour of the ridge. A grass tennis court and stone chairs and tables all sounded very nice. He had named the sanatorium after the English physician Dr George Bodington whose 1840 book on tuberculosis was influential on treatment. The Bodington relied on the climate of the mountains and its outdoor chalets as essential elements in its palliative care of consumptives.

He would recount the long silent train trips up the mountain to the chilling yet healthier air. The anguish they faced each time seeing their beloved daughter, her beauty fading from her now thin and pale face. Margaret and Harry hated their father's graphic descriptions of the chronic coughing up of blood, the fever, night sweats, and weight loss. He described the seemingly endless reflective walks along cliffs shared by pleasure seekers, young lovers and happy families on outings to escape the city heat. These spectacles of rugged cliffs, The Three Sisters, deep yawning gorges and the abundance of flora and fauna, wasted on the Carlssons isolated in their grief. Her mother's prayers, so many hours of prayers and pleas to the Virgin Mary and her God.

Near the end they took her home, sitting helplessly as they listened to her coughing and fighting for every breath. Even on that torrid day in 1928 Lizzie was still begging her God, her knees racked with pain on the hard stone church floor in front of the colourful Madonna figure. The sight of her husband walking towards her, his head bowed in this place foreign to him, dredged from her a scream that should have woken the dead resting in the old disused graveyard where headstones dated back to the first white settlers of her adopted country.

Nothing could contain her external grief but Charlie through the whole ensuing funeral and wake stood frozen in his thoughts, emotions tearing away at this once proud and strong man.

He had accepted God's will when baby Marian died only hours after her birth. There was sadness at laying this sweet bundle to rest but they had another strong and happy child to console themselves. The loss of Irene was not the same. The breadth of memories, dreams and expectations of a wonderful life, 'Daddy, I don't want to die', how could anyone forget those words. Scratched, ripped, burnt into every dream. Charlie withdrew to his shed and though externally to workmates and friends he was unchanged, to those who knew him there was a difference, a sadness that would never leave his eyes.

Chapter 20

The start of the dark years from war to war

The First World War had no real impact on the Carlssons. Charlie was still technically a Swedish citizen but had become naturalised, changing his official name to Charles Carlson in 1904. With an overseer's position at the docks ensuring supplies moved as quickly as possible, his participation as a soldier was never questioned, well not by his family or anyone who knew him personally.

There was one occasion, however, when in 1914 the police arrived, guns drawn, at the family's home. It was during the housewarming party for their new home in Leichhardt. The police had been informed that Charlie was German and thus should be put in one of the internment camps set up to house German citizens and thus possible enemies. As Charlie was at work late it was Lizzie that they had questioned. However, after she had explained about Charlie's heritage, his strategic position at the docks and produced the appropriate documents they let slip during the conversation that it was a neighbour across the road and two doors down who had contacted them.

Like a cobra striking or a she wolf protecting her mate, Lizzie flew out the door at a screaming pitch. The police watched, bemused. There were stories for years of the argument that followed, the volume of which brought the whole street out to listen. Mrs Martin had been jealous of Lizzie as she did have fine clothes and jewellery and acted the lady, but Lizzie scorned was a formidable force and within a week the Martins were gone, "to look after her sick sister in Brisbane", or so the story went.

Charlie in the short time they had been there was well known and very popular in the street. He was the first to help anyone in need thus all considered him a kind and gentle man. He had been in most of their houses fixing things or with small handmade gifts as a present on any of their children's birthdays. Mrs Martin had crossed the line; there was no sympathy for her from any quarter.

The first significant Australian action of the war was the Australian Naval and Military Expeditionary Force's landing on Rabaul on the 11th of September 1914. The force took possession of German New Guinea and the islands of the Bismark Archipelago. The 9th of November sinking of the German light cruiser *SMS Emden* by the Australian light cruiser *HMAS Sydney* in the Cocos Islands was another significant call to war. The event created hysteria about a possible German naval attack and fired up community concern. People wanted to do their bit, so reporting any possible German interests became common. In the case of Mrs Martin, the allegation was personal, not political.

Charlie had friends who were of German origins. Some, though Australian citizens, had been interned in Holsworthy near Liverpool and another at the old Berrima gaol. The camps were referred to as DOJ (Department of Justice) Camps. Those interned were not only German nationals but also those of recent German descent. As they were now considered to be enemy aliens, many had their homes and property seized by the government. This was allowed by the 1914 War Precautions Act and internees could be held without trial. Since it was impossible to intern all enemy aliens, as by 1914 it is estimated there were over 100,000 German descendants in Australia, the government pursued a policy of selective internment. They targeted the leaders of the German Australian Community and pastors of the Lutheran church. Internees at the camps formed management committees, theatre and art groups, self-education classes and cafés. Despite this many of the internees suffered from depression and anxiety. The Australian government tried to offer reasonable conditions hoping that Germany would look after Australian prisoners of war.

Germans in Australia also found their schools and churches were closed, German music was banned, German foods were renamed, and place names were also changed such as Blumberg became Birdwood, Germantown became Holbrook and German Creek became Empire Bay. Throughout Australia many German families changed their names to stop harassment. Charlie had already chosen to do the same. Like many seamen from Scandinavian and

European countries he had chosen to anglicise his name, as he had noted that some who didn't were treated with deep suspicion.

As part of the community, Charlie and his family were saddened by the thought of over 330,000 Australians serving in the war as sailors, soldiers, airmen and nurses. Though the papers covered major events Lizzie and Charlie talked about the terrible things these people were facing, the injured, the dying and the trauma that a battle field must create. They were heartbroken hearing about family, friends and neighbours who had loved ones missing or confirmed killed. Many of Charlie's contacts were divided on the need or right to have young men conscripted, in a war that he and others felt had more to do with protecting Britain and their empire rather than the needs of his Australia.

Australia's own Defence Act precluded using conscription for overseas military service as opposed to home defence. In his mind he knew that his new land was part of the empire but felt the costs were too high, a complete loss of a nation's ability to control their own destiny. It had been Britain who had declared war on Germany on behalf of Australia. His labour press reinforced this, writing that the only people who would benefit from the slaughter and carnage of a war were the plutocrats (wealthy) and profiteers. He had told Lizzie that he believed Australia should have been like his homeland, Sweden, which had attempted to remain neutral but asserted its right to free trade including much needed food imports from Germany. This the Allied forces had stopped, resulting in severe food shortages in Sweden. Eventually Sweden had been forced to agree to stop exports to Germany and allow a large part of their merchant fleet to be put at the Allies' disposal. Charlie felt in some ways the same thing was happening here. Markets for key exports, such as wool, were immediately lost and there was soon a chronic shortage of ships to carry Australian goods.

The government chose to fund the war by increasing note (money) issue, placing an inflationary pressure that resulted in a rapid rise in the cost of living. Charlie watched as the new prices for food put essentials out of the reach of many. Charlie's trade unions had voluntarily limited their actions with the country locked in war but by 1917 the economy had reached a point that a relatively minor dispute in a New South Wales Tramways Workshop triggered strikes in sympathy to their cause along the eastern seaboard. Through lockouts and use of scab labour, the unions were defeated but this had created a deepening divide between the layers of the society.

Lizzie no longer considered herself Irish though many of her relatives did. She knew that at the outbreak of the war, most Irish people, regardless of their religion or nationalist beliefs, backed what they considered the British war. Ireland had its own regiments and over 200,000 men from Ireland fought with 30,000 being killed. In the vein of Charlie's beliefs, her family were pleased to hear that in 1916, the Irish republicans had taken the opportunity of being in a war to proclaim an independent Irish Republic, free to govern its own destiny. She was not so happy to find this had resulted in an armed rebellion in Dublin, in which Germany had attempted to help. Her brother Martin had several years later told her how at the end of the war Irish republicans had won the Irish general elections and declared independence that resulted in the 1919 Irish War of independence. She was saddened by the thought of ex-servicemen who had fought in trenches next to each other now having to take sides and fight each other on their own soil. This conflict between the Irish Republican Army, IRA and British forces resulted in the partition of Ireland.

Regardless of their sentiments towards the participation in war, Lizzie and Charlie helped where they could. They donated money to help others during the war, part of the fourteen million pounds (about $1.3billion in current money) that was raised. Lizzie volunteered at a military convalescent home for injured returned service personnel, she knitted warm woollen socks and packed boxes of comforts from home to be sent to the soldiers. These contained tinned food, magazines, soap, matches and tobacco, ANZAC biscuits, knitted scarves and socks, toothbrush and shaving gear, tea and coffee, chewing gum, sewing repair kit, candles and chocolate. In later years Lizzie laughed when she heard that the Central Prisoner of War Committee in London, through a French commission, sent WW1 French prisoner of war packages that included potted chicken, various pâtés and a bottle of wine.

Working on the docks, Charlie knew the truth of the first shots fired in anger by the British Empire forces. At

12.10 a.m. when the news of the war had just reached the Australian government, the troops at Fort Nepean in Victoria fired shots across the bows of the German merchant ship *Pfalz*, forcing the ship to surrender. He also watched the first Australian Naval and Military Expeditionary Force of 1500 men leave Sydney to capture German New Guinea. Then in November the first contingent of the Australian Imperial Force leaving for Egypt. But not all domestic war organisation went well. In 1916 a newspaper headline read, "14,000 troops riot, sack city, in Australia", "Soldier riot: do $US two million damage" and "Australian recruits are in wild riot". After leaving their camps near Liverpool they rampaged through the streets of Sydney smashing windows of anyone with a foreign sounding name, including Italian restaurants, an ally of Australia in the war. Though about a thousand soldiers were court martialled and either gaoled or discharged, many were still sent overseas to fight.

The family like all in their street, and in most streets of the city, celebrated the end of the war and looked forward to happier times. The announcement of the armistice in November 1918 saw the news spread rapidly and from their home in Leichhardt they could hear the sound of steam whistles on ferries and locomotives in full blast. The shrill sent a shudder down the spine, a good tingle, excitement mixed with relief.

At about eight p.m. Charlie took Lizzie and the four children still living at home, into the city centre. George, Pitt, Elizabeth, all the major streets were gridlocked with crowds who had armed themselves with flags, fireworks and noise-makers, the latter so loud conversation was almost impossible as the commotion drowned out any attempt even with raised voice. It was nearly dawn when they returned home tired but exhilarated.

The following year was to have two major setbacks for the Carlssons and many of their maritime linked relatives.

Their daughter Irene who was now eight came home from school complaining about a headache and pain. Lizzie immediately put her to bed and sent Maria to fetch the doctor. They were shocked when Dr Ferguson walked through their front door wearing a gauze mask.

'I'm sorry, Lizzie, she's the third today, you know they're closing the schools?'

'What is it?' Lizzie demanded.

'I'm afraid it's a sickness that they are calling the Spanish flu. It's a type of influenza; it's a bad one, even worse than the one Charlie had a few years ago.'

Irene would recover but the flu would take six thousand lives in New South Wales. As it had spread, restrictions were introduced to limit contact. Schools, churches and places of entertainment were closed and instructions were issued that people travelling by public transport should wear gauze masks, all too late for the Carlssons. Eleven-year-old Francis also got sick but the symptoms were less severe and when his fever eventually broke he also recovered.

The disease did take the young lives of several family and close friends. As if her own, the loss of each child, though part of a wider community grief and beyond their control, was at the time more than Lizzie felt she could take. She cried uncontrollably for days as if her world had ended, but when her son became ill, she had quickly channelled her grief into fighting for his life. A twenty-four hour vigil, quietly watching and praying, was shared between Charlie and herself, their exhaustion masked for the sake of their family.

Family funerals, such as that for her nephew, had become small family ceremonies as the fear of the epidemic spreading had put the city into severe panic. There was no procession or gathering for a family wake. The three vehicle convoy that drove to the cemetery did so in almost secrecy. There was no viewing of the body and other children were not in attendance at the cold lonely graveside, only a handful of people allowed to see them at rest. Lizzie felt a sense of guilt, a foolish emotion, but when people turned and covered their faces as the funeral car drove past, she wanted to call out, 'They're dead, they can't hurt you. They're dead, at least show this beautiful child some respect,' but all that came out was a soft and diminishing, 'They're dead, they're dead, they're gone.' Then nothing for days but silent tears.

It wasn't the first time that influenza had occurred in the colonies. It was first noted in 1820 and reported in the *Sydney Almanac*. While influenza was common most winters, pandemic were not, including one in 1890s.

However, the most devastating pandemic was that of 1918–19. That pandemic was often called the Spanish Flu. Not because it started there but it was an area where it spread quickly. Unlike previous flu epidemics that seemed to mainly affect the very young and old with weaker immune systems, the Spanish Flu mostly affected healthy young adults between the ages of fifteen and thirty-five. Eventually about forty percent of the country's population were to fall ill with around 15,000 deaths. Some Aboriginal communities recorded a mortality rate of over fifty per cent. The virus had spread rapidly around the world as soldiers returned from active service in the war.

Charlie knew that the government had tried to take steps to prevent the illness entering the country. As an overseer on the docks he had been told about the Australian Quarantine Service and asked to help monitor the arrival of ships. The regulations had been put in place on the 17th of October 1918 after outbreaks in New Zealand and South Africa, both with major ports on the way to Australia's ports. It didn't take long for the first reported cases to arrive. The *Mataram* from Singapore arriving in Darwin on the 18th of October, the first. Over the next six months the service intercepted three hundred and twenty-three vessels before they could land; one hundred and seventy-four were carrying the infection.

The Commonwealth Government had also set up a Commonwealth Serum Laboratory during the war and it developed its first influenza vaccine against pneumonic influenza in 1918. This proved only partly effective in preventing death in inoculated adults. The government also established guidelines to be followed in each state regarding emergency hospital and quarantine camps, vaccination depots, ambulance services and public awareness programs. Tension flared between states as Victoria delayed the announcement of cases in Melbourne and the other states blamed Victoria for the spread of flu to their states. By the end of 1919, the influenza pandemic was over. Though it had been estimated that over eighteen million people had been killed during the First World War, up to a hundred million had died from the influenza pandemic.

Another impact was the 1919 strike by the Seamens' Union. This meant the closure of the docks and the loss of many jobs. Charlie found this hard, making decisions as to who would go was never easy to him, refusing people employment was against his very nature but he too had a family to think of. The strike was mainly about pay and conditions but the strikers were also concerned with the risk that the influenza posed to the seafarers.

Charlie and his Coal Lumpers' Union were not the focus of the industrial action. The Seamen's Union was on strike between May and August. It was actually a successful strike against arbitration, the national industrial court system, first established in 1904. Arbitration was opposed by the socialist element in the union. For three months the Seamen's Union defied the Commonwealth government's attempts to force them into arbitration. The seafarers wanted a 35 shilling a month increase, plus three shillings for overtime payments for any Sunday at sea. There was also outrage that the government had not met its commitment to pay seafarers a war bonus. The seamen also demanded sick payment for any time the ship was in quarantine and life insurance to provide for their families if they were killed by the flu. As coastal shipping was the main way of transporting goods, shortages occurred very quickly. The conservative Nationalist Federal government with Billy Hughes as prime minister tried to force the workers back to court. However the strike had brought almost all coastal shipping and a large percentage of international shipping to a halt. For Charlie no ships meant no coal lumping. Though the seafarers won gains Charlie understood this to be another example of class conflict. The seafarers fought for sick pay but the bosses and government were more concerned about maintaining profits.

Chapter 21

Jan Erik Carlsson

On 20th September 1920 Jan Erik Carlsson arrived in Australia as a crew member on an American ship. He was on his way to 63 Kent Street, Millers Point, where his younger brother Carl August Carlsson and family were living on a previous visit. He gave a loud bang on the door and called out but the door was opened by an apprehensive young girl. When Jan, in his heavily accented voice, asked to speak to Charles, the little girl slammed the door and yelled for her mother. He heard what turned out to be Maggie Carlson put on the door chain then open the door just a crack. Jan quickly apologised and explained he was looking for the family of his brother Carl Carlsson.

Maggie smiled and said in her own strongly accented Irish voice, 'You mean Charlie Boy.' Turning she called out to whoever was in the house, she said, 'It's Charlie's brother.'

She opened the door and ushered him in. Maggie directed him down the hall and into the kitchen area. Three other faces appeared who turned out to be Norman aged eight, Thelma, seven and Francis, five. The older child who had met him at the door was instructed to make tea, then introduced as Isabel, her eleven-year-old. Maggie identified herself as the younger sister of Charlie's wife Lizzie, by four years, and said that she had also married a Swedish sailor, Gustave Wilhelm Carlsson. They had moved into this house in 1916 when Lizzie and Charles moved into a house they had bought in Leichhardt. Maggie explained they had lived in several smaller rented houses in Millers Point at 58 High Street, 34 Lower Fort Street and even a few doors down at number 73 Kent Street, where another child, Roy, had died as a baby in 1911.

The children were delighted when Jan reached into his sailor sack and pulled out some cloth and from it withdrew a number of small animal figures made of green stone, which Jan called jade. Maggie objected but Jan assured her he had plenty of gifts which he had brought with him from his travels. In his broken English, he said, 'These I picked up in the markets at Shanghai.'

Over tea and some cake he told the children of his time in Egypt, southern Africa and the Orient. His exaggerated tales beguiled not only the children but Maggie. There was also something seductive in his voice, the hard life of a sailor sounding so fascinating.

Before he left for Charlie's home he gave Maggie a piece of silk cloth. Though she thought it was more likely he bought it from a street hawker, Jan told the children it was from the Imperial Palace in Peking. They were amazed by its bright colours with a large red dragon design in the centre.

'Dragons are important to the Chinese, they believe that dragons can offer protection to your home. Unlike European dragons that breathe fire, Chinese dragon breathe clouds. This red dragon,' he held up the cloth, 'is a symbol of good fortune.'

Jan gauged that his small audience wanted more.

'Some dragons are also blue and green and they give you good health and peace, however, a black dragon,' he pulled a scary face raising his hands above his head, 'is vengeance, getting even for wrong doings. I like the yellow dragon, it's a symbol of good fortune and power.'

At that Jan pulled up his sleeve to reveal a small tattoo of a dragon in black ink that had some yellow colouring.

'This dragon is to protect me at sea, to ward off sea monsters and pirates.'

The children gasped at the thought of large monsters attacking ships, or being captured by pirates and made to walk the plank.

'See how his head looks like the cross between a camel and a lion but his large eyes are those of a dragon. He has a long neck like a snake but his paws have sharp claws like a tiger. But don't be scared, Chinese dragons are not vengeful, they are wise and powerful.'

Though Maggie thought it was time for Jan to continue on his way to Charlie's, the children were having such a good time so she got Jan a beer and sat with them to listen to the rest of his tale.

'In China, a long time ago, they had an emperor, he was a type of king, like our King Gastaf the Fifth.'

The children looked at their mother as the only real king they had heard about was at school and he was the British King George V. She just smiled again, Anders had mentioned his Swedish king, and being Irish Maggie didn't think much of the British monarchy anyway. She could remember that some English law had made whoever was king of England also the legal king of Ireland and that Henry VIII was the first to hold the joint title. Jan continued.

'Who they thought was descended from a dragon. His name was Yandi and he was more powerful than the other leaders so his armies were able to conquer his enemies and create the country China.'

Maggie smiled, she had no idea whether Jan was telling the truth or just another story.

'Lots of people in China believe that Yandi was one of their ancestors, thus they are also descended from dragons.'

'Like our ancestors were Vikings?' Norman asked in an excited voice.

Maggie interrupted, she could see this would become tales of the Vikings, and the children got enough of that from their Uncle Charlie who was also a great storyteller.

'Children, Jan has to get to his family's home, it's getting late and Aunty Lizzie does not like surprises, like an unexpected guest arriving just before dinner.'

She felt guilty saying this in front of Jan, but it was true, of all her siblings Lizzie was the most black and white about everything. Added to this was the fact that nine days earlier Lizzie had given birth to their third son Harry, both well but new baby and unexpected visitor was going to be a challenge even for her. Maggie had chosen not to mention the birth and fortunately none of her children had either. She thought if she had, Jan may have gone looking for a boarding house rather than the expected stay with his brother.

Maggie accompanied him to Leichhardt by tram but with her wonderful sense of humour suggested he walk slowly up the street while she rushed ahead into the house pretending to be out of breath as a man had been following her. Charlie rushed outside to confront the offender only to find his brother waiting for him.

Jan was to stay with Charlie and his family till he left on a ship bound for San Francisco on the 1st of October 1920. Sadly the family was never to hear from him again. On his stay Jan was to be made godfather to baby Harry and his visit was welcomed as Maria, now twenty one, had taken over the role of house manager while her mother Lizzie cared for the baby.

Lizzie tolerated the visit; the only point of confrontation revolved around the evenings when Charlie, his brothers Jan and Anders and Lizzie's brother in law Gustave Carlsson would sit in the kitchen, and speaking in their native Swedish tongue shared memories and experience. As Jan and Anders smoked their carved curved pipes, Gustave, who they called Gus, had his hand rolled cigarettes and Charlie smoked cigars, the room quickly filled with the strong odour of tobacco. Normally when

Charlie had a cigar it was in his workshop or shed in the back garden.

As with his visit to Maggie's home, on the night of his arrival at Charlie's Jan produced an array of exotic gifts for the family. Maria and Irene were given ivory hair combs with carved animal designs that Jan had got in southern Africa. Esma, aged five and Margaret, three, were both given Chinese dolls in elaborate silk clothing and Francis who was twelve, a bone handle knife with ivory sheath also from Jan's visit to Africa. To her amazement and delight he had brought Lizzie a string of black pearls and Charlie a pair of book ends, black mahogany elephants with ivory tusks. When objections were raised about the generosity of the gifts Jan simply stated he was fifty-four, never was and never would marry, thus he had lots of spare cash to do with what pleased him.

As Anders' wife had died in 1906, in addition to the matching bookends the same as he gave Charlie, Jan also gave Anders a black pearl tie stick pin in memory of his wife. It was perhaps this thoughtful gift that remained the strongest memory of his brothers and brother in law after he left.

Chapter 22

The last two

Margaret had a very close bond with her younger brother. He was like a live toy and she spent most of her time trying to help her oldest sister Maria look after what Margaret called the bub. This was not really appreciated by Lizzie,

'You're always under my feet, leave him alone, he was nearly asleep.'

The two of them were inseparable and Lizzie, who could not understand or cope with the losses that befell her, relied more and more on Margaret and Harry to look after each other. Being born close together they shared the same milestones throughout life. They were built-in best friends and allies, able to combine and unite in adversity or as a power play to get what they wanted.

Margaret was the first of the Carlsson children to be sent to a local government primary school. The break from her mother's strong belief in the benefit of a strong religious based education had resulted from the challenges and lack of support in relation to Esma's learning difficulties. Lizzie basically blamed the school for Esma's inability to read and write. After the family had moved to

Leichhardt, Irene was moved to Saint Fiacre Primary School, the four eldest having commenced their schooling at St Brigid's in Kent Street, Millers Point. Lizzie, like so many people in this time, felt that education was more important for boys thus paid for Carl and Francis to attend a local college, St Josephs in Rozelle. Irene, who had proven to be a gifted student, was eventually moved to Fort Street High to complete her education.

Margaret and in his turn Harry were enrolled in Orange Grove Public School. The school had opened in 1923 as a one room timber and canvas building in the rapidly expanding residential area of Leichhardt. Later this section of Leichhardt would be renamed Lilyfield. Margaret was in the first intake at the school and both children liked the school and their teachers. The one thing both resented was the days that they had to leave during school time and walk a long distance to the local Catholic church. This was made worse by the fact that the children who attended Saint Fiacre Primary sat in a group while they sat on their own to learn the catechism and prepare for First Communion and Confirmation. They felt they were being punished but the action was aimed at Lizzie and her decision to enrol them at the rival state school.

On completion of primary school Margaret attended Balmain High, doing her schooling in the Girls' Building, a three storey section of the school completed in 1915. Boys' classes were held in a separate building. Harry like his father loved practical activities especially working with timber, so was enrolled at Sydney Technical High School, Albion Street, Paddington.

Despite a series of tragic moments, Margaret and Harry had a relatively happy childhood. As young children they played together, Margaret's two favourite games being Viking warriors with toy wooden swords their father made and a game where she was a beautiful Swedish princess and Harry a young knight saving her from the castle where she was locked away. For this their father allowed them to use his work shed as their castle and built them a play area where Margaret kept her dolls and Harry his toys.

These games had developed from the stories that their father had told them about their Swedish history and the city of Uppsala.

'On the hill overlooking the town is a large castle with high walls, it used to be where the old royal family lived. They now live in Stockholm.'

Margaret wished she was a princess in that castle.

'Near the town are large mounds, buried in these are Viking kings and their long boats. These ships sailed all over the world and the Vikings were feared as great warriors. Wearing their helmets with horns, round shields, swords, axes and bows they would attack cities and towns taking the prizes of victory home to their villages.'

Both Margaret and Harry could visualise this. Charlie made models of long boats for his children and both of them had shields and horned helmets that had appeared as presents.

'There is a great cathedral with spires that reach to the sky, far larger than the one in Sydney, and buried in it are many generations of kings and queens. As you walk around it there are large carved stone statues of each of them and the whole ceiling has beautiful paintings. Everything is so old and solid, most built before white people even discovered that Australia was here.'

Margaret was inspired by his stories and wished they lived in this exciting city and decided that she would one day visit these wonderful places.

Though the youngest two may not have felt it, they were both very spoiled compared to the older children.

Besides the hours spent with Charlie, Margaret used to spend time watching her older sister Irene, who like many of her friends, was engulfed by the American style that they saw in the movies. She convinced her mother to allow her to wear short skirts and get a short hairstyle known as the Shingle. Music pervaded the house and they all clapped and laughed as Irene and her best friend and cousin Kathleen tried to learn the Charleston and the Blackbottom.

Lizzie would tut-tut and complain as they attempted to get her into the swing.

'I'm not doing those silly things; I'll leave it up to you young people.'

The chance of public and even private embarrassment was something that Lizzie would never accept.

In 1923 there was a new excitement in the Carlsson home as first radio stations 2FC and 2BL were established and the Carlssons were the first family in their street to purchase a receiver. Selected neighbours would come to their home to listen and Margaret was proud to invite her school friends around to see and hear this wonderful invention. Before long Francis had made himself a crystal set; he was now fourteen and very good with anything like that. Margaret had heard him talk about becoming an engineer and knew her father was proud that his son was so good at school and had ambitions of getting into a profession.

For Margaret and Harry Saturday morning meant jobs to do around the house but they accepted them eagerly for a reward was money to go to the local picture and a penny to buy a treat. Their mother would take them as it was only a short walk to The Molboura picture theatre in Norton Street and she both enjoyed and approved of the comedies that were screened during the afternoon sessions. She had never gone to an evening session, concerned about possible immoral content. So these afternoon silent movies, mainly imported comedies from America with stars like Buster Keaton, Harold Lloyd and Charlie Chaplin, became family favourites.

The outing was itself pleasurable as theatres being built were ornate, plush and flamboyant. Lizzie especially enjoyed the organ music and live stage show that the cinema often had before and with the film. It was at one of these that Margaret and Harry saw their mother truly laugh for the first time. Always reserved, she would smile at a joke or funny happening but during several of these comedies, in the darkness which offered a certain degree of anonymity, she laughed until tears were running down her face. She also held their hands, one sitting on each side of her, 'In case you might fight or talk during the movie.'

These were relatively happy memories. Ones you put at the front of your mind to obscure or hide reality.

Sometimes as a special treat their father would take them to Leichhardt stadium to watch the boxing and wrestling. He and his brother would sit up the front with large cigars and the children would be allowed to buy treats and they enjoyed any live entertainment that occurred between the matches. Lizzie did not approve of this violence and never attended.

'It's so vulgar and common,' was her favourite saying.

There was a close bond between these men from Sweden for once a month Andrew Carlsson, his son-in-law Herman Bogran (Peterson), Gustave Carlsson and Charlie Carlsson had an afternoon playing cards, cribbage being their game. Lizzie always set out two afternoon teas, leaving the men in the breakfast room, the ladies in the lounge room. When the game began, the door was firmly closed. The reason, the evil of tobacco, as even with the windows wide open, a cloud of smoke hovered over the table.

Harry loved these events. Between the competitive meeting of these four very quietly spoken, gentle men, Charlie would teach and practise with his son. However, on the occasion of the friends meeting, Harry was kept in the background. His Uncle Gustave, with his tin of cigarettes in one pocket, would also have a bag of hard boiled lollies in the other pocket. Halfway through the game he would pull out the lolly bag, call Harry over, give him one plus a pat on the head, tell him he was a good lad, and send him back to his corner.

When Margaret left school she gained employment in a Marcus Clark & Co department store that had been built on the corner of George and Harris Streets, built in 1909 and called The Hub. It is here she had met her two best friends, Monica and Constance.

Marcus Clark & Co had started in the Sydney suburb of Newtown in 1883 as a draper shop, and soon opened new stores in Marrickville and Bondi Junction. By 1896 they also had stores close to the centre of the city at Broadway and the corner of Harris Street near Railway Square. This store had become known as the flat-iron because of its angular shape. Though there were many department store chains developing in Sydney, Marcus Clark was stocked with less expensive wares catering for the average family. The nine storey structure at Railway Square was one of the tallest buildings in Sydney and had been built on that particular location as originally the railway network ended at Central so all those leaving the station for connections to the city would walk past the new store. The store was also the first to introduce the concept of customer credit purchases particularly for people on lower incomes, which they called the Gradual Payment Scheme.

Charlie had bought Margaret a car as an eighteenth birthday present, a four cylinder Chevrolet tourer, and at every opportunity the girls headed off for an outing. Harry was included in most of these, especially when they were to one of the National Parks, as bush walking was a preferred exercise. The Royal National Park was a favourite with its coastal tracks and amazing ocean views.

In 1937 Margaret changed her employment to another city store, David Jones. Here she took on the role of a buyer, selecting the items that the store would sell in their children's wear department. Part of the move had been influenced by her friend Monica who now worked at David Jones and was a member of the stores Dajonians Repertory Society, a staff club amateur performance group. Their plays were performed both at the David Jones theatrette and also in some independent theatres like the St James Hall.

Though not particularly thinking herself talented, she enjoyed the fun of rehearsals that was part of putting on light comedies. The company had employed a permanent producer, Carl Francis, and presented six plays a year. Margaret especially enjoyed the troupe's productions of some of John Priestley's comedies. Her favourites included *Laburnum Grove*, a play about trying to get rid of sponging relatives by declaring you are a master forger, and *When We Are Married* where three couples, all married on the same day, discover they are not legally married and find themselves re-evaluating their marriages. Her last performance with the group was in the production of *Call it a Day*. This was a play written by British writer, Dodie Smith. The play had been originally performed in the Globe Theatre in London and been a huge success. In 1937 it had been made into a Hollywood movie featuring Olivia de Havilland. The plot revolves around a day in the life of a dysfunctional family, something that Margret considers was the norm for most families. Hers certainly had their skeletons in the cupboards, the black sheep. She had played the younger sister, a teen who moons dreamily about the perfect man. Margaret wanted the perfect man, hadn't met many yet, but was hopeful.

Harry left school when he was fifteen but as the world economy was only just crawling out of the Great Depression, the only apprenticeship he could get in cabinet making was at Hurstville. This entailed a twenty six kilometre push bike ride each way, thus he left in the dark and returned home in the dark. Charlie was unhappy with this arrangement and through a friend who shared a common interest in model ship making found him a position at Corkhill and Land in Chippendale. On Friday nights after work Harry would go into the city and meet up with Margaret, have a cup of tea, sometimes go to a show, and for a while they did dancing lessons together.

Chapter 23

Sydney 1929

In the spring of 1929 when her mother would normally have been busy in her flowerbeds of their Leichhardt home things were silent. The garden was always a mass of colour as both Lizzie and her youngest child Harry had what people call green thumbs and anyone who visited agreed that whatever they planted seemed to grow bigger and brighter than in anyone else's garden in Sydney.

Charlie's work-shed, his pride and joy, a sanctuary from life's trials, stood behind the timber and fibro garage was still and lifeless.

The house in Ramsey Street was similar in appearance to number two, four, eight, twelve and fourteen. Number ten was a smaller home on a smaller block. These were large double brick homes that were very different from some of the older style homes on the other side of the street. Theirs was a spacious and well-appointed residence, the most Spartan facility being the laundry or washhouse attached to the back of the home with gas copper, a trough, a scrubbing board and mangle or hand ringer. Though Charlie had tried to convince Lizzie to get a washing and ironing woman, saying, 'There are many women who need the work, impoverished by widowhood, spinsterhood, desertion or with a husband who drinks,' she flatly refused.

Thus, Monday was washing day, a full day's work, the copper filled and lit, the clothes immersed, boiled, and removed with a copper stick for rinsing, blueing, wringing and pegging out. Dirty work clothes often had to be soaked overnight and rubbed vigorously on the scrubbing board. When finished the copper had to be bailed out, scoured and vinegared clean. Tuesday was then ironing and airing day with almost everything being dampened and starched before ironing. Sheets, underwear, even socks, Lizzie ironed it all.

Behind the family vegetable garden was a large tract of still vacant land that acted as a makeshift football field, cricket pitch and battleground for the local children. Its most infamous time was leading up to Empire Night on the 24th of May, Queen Victoria's birthday. All the neighbourhood children would form into war camps. In addition to the collegial activity of fossicking for old wood and other flammable materials to build the largest bonfire possible, all spare time was devoted to building forts with fighting trenches for the great cracker war. Soon after dusk, thousands of bonfires were set alight around the city, the glows being visible from all vantage points in the city. For hours the night sky was punctured by rockets, showers of sparks and coloured stars. But that was not the best bit. Children ran and shrieked in the shadows, pockets full of bungers ready to be lit and thrown at unwary enemy.

All the Carlsson families met for the occasion and Charlie's brother Anders always managed to purchase huge bags of fireworks wholesale through a Chinese importer. The wars seemed to grow larger each year, the planning for the forts more elaborate. Though their parents knew, and many disapproved and tried to ban their child from participating, somehow the encounter was allowed. That was, however, until the year that Lizzie's middle son Francis had to be rushed to hospital in an ambulance after the fireworks exploded in his pocket. The family suspected that a spark had fallen into his trousers, but his gang laid the blame on the warring combatants for dropping a lighted tom-thumb cracker in his pocket. Regardless, Francis was left with a permanent burn scar on his thigh and hip and any future cracker wars were banned.

It was also the last of the large Empire Night parties as Lizzie had blamed Charlie's brother for supplying the bungers and the whole evening ended in an enormous argument. This was reinforced by articles in the following day's *Daily Telegraph* that reported hundreds of frightened residents calling fire brigades to put out fires in streets and vacant lots close to homes and factories. The report referred to "swarms" of children hampering firemen, calling them names, standing on their hoses and pelting them with crackers. Lizzie was not going to condone her family being part of this hooliganism.

The house itself was cool in summer and due to the five open grate fireplaces, very cosy in the colder winter months. The three main bedrooms had French doors leading onto the verandas, very ornate fireplaces topped with large gilt mirrors, and each room contained a dressing table vanity, a strange combination of matching hand basin, water jug, soap holder, small mirror and cupboards on each side.

The front door of the house was of solid timber with leadlight and there were matching leadlight panels on either side depicting a country scene, each with a shamrock to ward off evil. Over the door hung a horseshoe, a cold iron object to protect the house and a wreath of rowan and herbs. Past the two front bedrooms was a large lounge room containing a heavy carved mantlepiece with some of its sections rising to the ten foot ceiling. On this was kept fine porcelain from China, alabaster from Karnak on the River Nile and crystal and other treasures from Ireland and the various countries Charlie had visited as a seaman. He had been fascinated by their beauty and delicateness and became a collector. This, his wife happily continued adding to the showcase throughout their married life. His favourite pieces however, had little monetary value but were priceless in terms of memories. These were two china dogs that had belonged to his grandmother and from his earliest childhood he could remember, like so many other families in the Swedish sailing communities, them being used as a sign. The dogs sat in the front windows and if they faced outwards they were waiting for a sailor's return, if facing inwards it meant that he was home safely. Charlie had been given these as a parting gift, they had sat for so many years looking outwards when his grandfather had not returned, presumed lost at sea in one of the gales that whipped the North Sea into a foaming frenzy.

This room also had French doors leading out into a small, meticulously manicured garden, in a formal European style. Adjoining this was the dining room with a large bulky extension table, eight brocade and thickly padded balloon back chairs and a leather settee with a carved wooden backrest that made it the most comfortable piece of furniture in the house. The room contained a large fireplace with removable cast iron grate and Lizzie's prize possession an ornately carved sideboard that covered one complete wall.

This front portion of the house was off limits to the children, their mother's domain. Even the children's access to the house was only allowed down the side passage, entering through the kitchen in case mud might mark the precious Persian carpet squares. Her father was allowed through the front as long as he was wearing his house shoes. Certain guests, especially relatives, were also quickly informed to leave their shoes at the front door, that's if any risked visiting through this special portal.

The next central corridor passed two more bedrooms and a bathroom with striking black and white tiles and a large claw legged bath above which stood a chip wood heater to provide hot water. Next to the bathroom was a special place, a large walk-in pantry, shelves filled with homemade jams, pickles, biscuits, and dozens of bottles of homemade ginger beer which sometimes exploded while fermenting. These pantries were an essential feature of most modern homes of the time as little food was precooked or tinned or packaged and perishable food was bought in small quantities as required, especially in summer. This to the Carlsson children was a real Aladdin's cave. The pantry was strictly off limits to the younger children, only making Margaret and Harry more determined to get in by pulling a chair over to the door so they could reach the bolt. Success was well rewarded, being caught very painful, with a clip over the ear from their mother or the ever ready leather strap around the legs or bottom. There were no "spare the rod and spoil the child" issues in the Carlsson home, Lizzie was a firm believer in corporal punishment. Charlie would disappear for a long walk or into his garden shed when confrontation between Lizzie and one of her children was imminent.

The breakfast room with its adjoining kitchen and laundry was where the young members of the house and their friends spent most of their time. A long wooden table with six wooden stools proved ideal for playing bobs, ping pong, cards, doing homework and eating everyday meals.

Lizzie was a plain cook but having to prepare twenty-seven meals a day, as she always insisted all her family had cooked breakfasts and a substantial packed lunch, was about all she had time for. Each week with few exceptions the menu was the same. Friday as with all good Catholic families was fish, sometimes with home grown potato made into wedges, other times with vegetables also grown in their own garden. As most of the family had sport and other commitments on Saturday meals were lighter, usually cold meats, bread and cheese. Sunday the traditional baked dinner with Monday, bubble and squeak, leftover meat from Sunday cooked with potato and cabbage. Tuesday the rabbit man came in his horse-drawn cart and dressed the number of rabbits needed for the evening meal. Wednesday was fresh tripe from the butcher shop and Thursday sausages. There was always some type of sweet each night or homemade bread with a block of strong tasting cheese. In the winter months a large black iron pot was always on the wood burning stove with various types of soups on hand for after sport or when friends came to visit.

Like most families this room also contained the medicine chest and the children could vividly remember the array of homemade remedies that it held. This was always more than a memory, instant nausea, every time the children thought about them, those past tastes would swell back into their mouth and the smells flooding their nostrils making them shiver with displeasure. A cough mixture was made from block liquorice, linseed and water, boiled and cooled, or for a quick fix four or six drops of kerosene or Friar's Balsam on a spoon with sugar. A sore throat meant six drops of iodine in a small glass of milk. In the case of boils a very hot linseed poultice wrapped in lint was applied, or Bates Salve, a black compound that had to be melted on lint and applied when hot, both very painful. Despite all these Margaret and Harry remembered what they considered the cruellest of all, when each of the children was forced to take opening medicine every Saturday morning. This Epsom salts, castor oil or senna tea leaves concoction made them almost ill just smelling it. After this they would head off to the pictures or for an outing with the family but as their mother would not allow them to use public toilets, saying, 'They're full of disease,' it became an agonising rush to get home after the show.

Margaret smiled when she remembered how one afternoon on the way home her younger brother Harry ran ahead of her and was hit by a motor bike as it raced out of a neighbour's driveway driven by Robbie Martin. Harry was taken to hospital with a badly bruised arm and leg but the rider, who was drunk and considered by most as the local lout and criminal type, had a broken leg. For Margaret the irony was that when her mother arrived at the hospital, rather than consoling her injured son, she hit him with a verbal tirade about running away from his sister and causing harm to another man even if it was, 'That woman's son.' Margaret remembered Harry's sad face and how upset his mother's reaction had made him.

Lizzie Carlsson was a good Christian woman. Her family never wanted for anything and even during the depression were well fed and clothed and at all times had many advantages that other families did not. In saying that, her children could not remember many signs of love, compassion or even understanding from her. Their mother was a very private person with few close friends. Thinking back Margaret could not remember her mother ever going into a shop to buy anything. In those days except for meat and groceries everything else was delivered to the door at least once a week. As the grocer was a distant Irish relative her mother would just send an order with one of the children for him to be delivered, the same with the butcher. So, other than the church, social work and a few family outings, her whole world appeared to revolve around her family and home.

She was completely devoted to her Catholic religion, working tirelessly at any church function or fundraising activity including St Vincent's de Paul, Boystown, and after World War One, for returned servicemen. She would never accept an official position, rarely attended meetings, always preferring to work quietly in the background. Her energy and drive surprised many; even her own sisters referred to Lizzie as "the lady of the Carlsson family". Perhaps no one really understood her or had the chance to get close enough to try. She set herself such high standards that others might not comprehend, but unfortunately although she lived by them they caused constant friction as no one else ever reached them. She was not a forgiving person and if anyone spoke ill of her or her family they were not welcome back in the home, this included relatives. Perhaps she was too protective or controlling of everyday life going on around her family but that was all she knew; it was how she had been brought up by her own tyrannical parents. However, her fanatical pursuit of religious idealism resulted in moral criticism of evil ways and had often led to her children only understanding half-truths or having a complete lack of understanding on some topics.

In different ways each of her children was fond of her and though she seemed not able to directly show love, she conveyed her feelings in many other ways. She taught her children to respect their elders, to always help others, to maintain a high standard of appearance; yes, she did the best she could.

Charlie Carlsson was a quiet, gentle man who rarely raised his voice in anger. Yet as his children grew he would just have to look up, shake his head and they knew to be quiet even though he had never raised a hand to them. Though almost complete opposites, his devotion to his wife was always evident and when her Irish paddy was at its most devastating level his calm, heavily accented voice could be heard above the roar.

'Yes, dear, there is no need to worry, we can work it out.'

There always appeared to be masses of neighbourhood children in their home as Charlie mended shoes, fixed bikes, and made kites and small toys, especially little sailing boats and brightly painted wooden horses, a symbol of his Swedish ancestry.

He also told the most wonderful stories and groups of children would sit and listen as he talked about the sea, the tales of his shipwreck and his homeland.

Though from a coastal village, his father had not wanted him going to sea, so he had lived with an uncle in Gamla Uppsala, a craftsman specialising in the art of goldsmith who had become a recluse on his family farm. He had grown up in an environment of Gothicism which glorified the history and hope for the future of the Swedish nation. So his stories were of Gamla Uppsala, the centre of the mythical Atlantis, the primeval source of all human culture and science. He talked of ancient gods of Greece and Rome and how they had developed from the north such as Jupiter, a distortion of Old Swedish Jo-pitter another name for the god Thor, and Hercules from the Norse Har-Kalle or "army leader". He told of Odin, the most powerful god, the god of death and war, of magic and art; and of Thor, the god of thunder and lightning, of wind and rain, who helped and supported the farmers and who Thursday was named after.

He would recount his own childhood stories of the great Viking kings being descendants from Ubbo, great-grandson of the biblical Noah and that it was these ancient leaders who spread out and became the founders of the Roman, Greek and Egyptian Empires.

He would tell of Eric the Red and his men in open longboats battling the seas and all its ocean monsters in order to find riches and new lands. He would describe the huge earthen mounds near his uncle's home that were the burial places of the kings, buried in their long boats full of treasure for the afterlife, "Valhalla".

These stories were told to the local children, more as adventures than history but with his own children, especially his daughter Irene, he would add greater "historic fact".

'At the famous temple of Ubsola (Uppsala) not far from Sigtuna the people worshiped the images of three gods. The priests would offer sacrifices on behalf of the people and every nine years there was a great feast. Everyone was required to attend, and they would offer the sacrificed heads of nine of every living male creature. The bodies were hung from a sacred tree near the temple, dogs, falcons, oxen, horses and men, hung together, seventy-two bodies in all.

'The Vikings were bold and adventurous but feared. Some churches had special prayers for protection, "God, deliver us from the fury of the Northman." It didn't work. The most feared of them was a warrior called Berserker, it's funny but in English they have the word berserk to describe a madman or someone acting wildly.' Charlie smiled. 'Yes, your ancestors left their mark on the world.'

His good Catholic wife certainly would not have approved of these tales, perhaps calling these pagan beliefs blasphemous, but it was his heritage and identity and he was proud of it and wanted his children to understand their cultural background.

Another family activity that Lizzie complained about but seemed to enjoy was the visits to the Grand Opera House. It had become the major venue for variety theatre and vaudeville acts. The Christmas pantomimes were particularly popular, especially the feature comedy duo Stiffy (Nat Phillips) and Mo (Roy Rene). Their act appealed to the audiences as it promoted the larrikin attitude of Australians, the emphasis on mateship, loyalty, and the refusal to bow to authority figures. In each show their characters usually portrayed life in a particular job such as plumbers, wharfies, waiters and bullfighters. There were the expected practical jokes and slap-stick humour but done in good taste.

Charlie and Lizzie could both remember the theatre being built in the early 1900s. It had originally been called the Adelphi Theatre, built on part of the old Paddy's Market site. It was one of four theatres built around the same time: the Lyric, the New Colonial on George Street and the Orpheum, but these were built as picture theatres. In 1932 the Grand Opera House was renamed the New Tivoli Theatre and became famous for its chorus girls, known as the Tivoli tappers.

Chapter 24

October 1929, the Wall Street Crash

Charlie was one of the fortunate ones. Life changed dramatically for many Australians, especially the working class. Many families lost everything. As with the strikes of 1919, his overseer's position assured his job. Each morning huge crowds of unemployed men pushed and clambered for daily work on gangs to unload ships as they arrived. Charlie and the other overseers could pick at will, only taking the strongest looking or people they knew were good workers. Thousands of disappointed and dejected men left the docks each day to attempt to find other avenues of eking out a living. Because the Australian economy depended so heavily on wool and wheat exports, and the overseas demand for these dried up very quickly, Australia was one of the worst affected countries in the world.

In the 1920s Prime Minister Stanley Bruce tried to lower Australia's five and a half million pound deficit by reducing government spending and people's wages. This became increasingly unpopular and in the 1929 election the Labor government of James Scullin gained power. His government raised taxes on imports and reduced migration. Nothing worked and in 1931 Joseph Lyons and his United Australia Party gained control. They reduced Commonwealth government spending.

As the papers showed, by 1933 the unemployment rate in Sydney was running at thirty two percent. Charlie, like most workers, had to take a pay cut but at the same time prices also fell. Fortunately having a large back garden, vegetable production was maximised and where possible surplus was dried or bottled. For the Carlssons the Great Depression was a time of austerity rather than poverty.

One of the saddest visual impacts for the Carlssons were neighbours moving out, selling their homes for whatever they could get and leaving. Loading what few possession they could stack into wagons or barrows, often asking families like the Carlssons who had employment if they wanted to buy anything. Charlie, soft by nature sometimes did, paying more than the item was worth. Lizzie refused and became annoyed at her husband.

Some did get help. Tommy next door lost his job early in 1929 and though feeling humiliated he joined the growing queue for rations. Tommy would take a sugar bag and head into the city to a centralised depot. He would have to line up for a ration ticket, collect the goods and because he had no money for fares, carry his sack home. Tommy was, however, lucky. He had been a good tenant and unlike many families whose landlords evicted people who could not pay, Tommy and his family were allowed to stay in their house. Charlie was kept informed by Tommy of his fight for survival and was pleased that the government had taken steps to support its people.

As the depression dragged on families like Tommy's were given dole coupons. These allowed them to get fixed amounts of goods through local bakers, butchers, grocers and milkmen. Out of interest Charlie asked how much Tommy got and was told the dole as a family man with two children was only eighteen shillings a week compared to Charlie's ten pounds per week. The term "susso" came into being, a colloquial expression for the sustenance relief rations. The term also inspired a popular children's song that upset Lizzie when she heard her daughter singing, reminding them of how fortunate they were compared to others.

We're on the susso now,
We can't afford a cow,
We live in a tent,
We pay no rent,
We're on the susso now.

It was often low-skilled workers and new migrants who found themselves camping out. Their dwellings were shanties, made of scraps of wood, corrugated iron, hessian and cardboard made waterproof with a mixture of lime and fat boiled in salt water. They relied on charity for survival in a society without a comprehensive welfare system. Suicide rates increased and over 40,000 men travelled around the country looking for work, along the way setting up small temporary towns. Fathers deserted their families and went on the track, becoming itinerant workers called swagmen. Others sadly took to drink and petty crime. In some homes women took in male boarders who were in work and daughters attempted some amateur prostitution. Working class children consistently left school at thirteen or fourteen and found they were sacked at sixteen as a business cost saving. Married women carried the greater domestic burden. Her unemployed husband would still expect her to cook and keep the house clean after working all day scrubbing floors to bring in some money.

Not all were willing to accept these handouts. Charlie saw many professional men working with pick and shovel, their hands wrapped in rags with blood coming through from the blisters below. Independence and pride were the most important things for many; they wanted to be able to pay cash not hand over a coupon. The time also saw the development of "jumping the rattler". In an attempt to find work, some men would jump onto moving trains to allow them to travel between locations quickly. Most only had a swag and worn-out shoes. Men who participated in this lifestyle were known as hoboes.

Perhaps those most affected were the indigenous population. Still not identified as Australian citizens, they were denied government pensions and food rations. As a result many were forced onto closed government reserves under intense surveillance of the Aboriginal Protection Board. Here the threat of having their children taken away was of real concern.

Families where possible made do with what they had. Mending, reusing and recycling became a necessity of life. Almost everyone saved zippers, buttons and other embellishments to re-stitch into different items of clothing. When clothing became too worn they were simply refashioned as quilts or cot covers.

Charlie tried to help where he could. His skill at shoe repair was welcomed by many families who could only afford the leather; he did the work for free. As things became harder Charlie also supplied the leather and did the work with vague promises of eventual payment, rarely kept. In his workshop he made wooden toys, giving them to the needy so parents had something to give their children on special occasions like birthdays and Christmas. His painstaking work assembling three and four masted fully rigged sailing ships in bottles became a treasured possession, gifts to his closest relatives. Sadly for Charlie he found this beloved relaxation and escape becoming harder all the time. He had seen a doctor about the increasing pains in his hands, especially his right hand. He had also noticed that his little finger and ring finger on his left hand had started to bend inward.

His doctor smiled saying, 'With an accent like yours and the name Carlsson I don't really need to look.'

Charlie was a bit taken back.

'It's very common in men from Scandinavia and Eastern Europe, it's called Dupuytren's syndrome and there's not much we can do about the deformity. Lots of men, and some women, tend to start developing it around fifty. Sadly it will get worse and your boys will most likely get it as well as it seems to be hereditary.'

Dr Dundas went on to explain that the syndrome had been known about for over two hundred years, originally described by a Swiss doctor, Felix Platter. The actual condition was named for a French surgeon, Baron Guillaume Dupuytren, who gave a well-documented lecture on retraced fingers in 1831.

'The condition affects the layer of tissue that lies under the skin. This will eventually create a thick cord that, as in your case, will pull one or more fingers into a bent position.'

Dr Dundas recommended hand flexing exercises to try and slow the bending and taking aspirin if the pain got too much. Charlie had never been fond of taking medications. He was more a suffer in silence type.

On the home front, one of the Carlssons' youngest children, Harry, recalled the interesting food of the time. Nothing was wasted, thus bread with dripping became a favourite. This consisted of the fat of cooked meat spread on homemade bread. Though the family traditionally had rabbit in their weekly food planning it became more commonly called poor man's chicken.

Mock foods became popular as creative cooks substituted ingredients with whatever was available and affordable. For the Carlssons this resulted in Lizzie creating an extensive range of meals based on the choko, a relatively tasteless green fruit, of the chayote vine, originally from South America. This climbing vine grew on the Carlsson's side fences, on the trellises that Charlie had erected, and covered an extensive roof area of Charlie's shed. The vines produced masses of fruit similar to a pear in shape and size. In the 1930s the Australian *Women's Weekly* published recipes for mock fish, mock pineapple and mock jam. Lizzie also used the choko as a pie filler, in jam to make it go further, as the basis of a vegetable soup and to make pickles.

Other popular soups were potato soup as again Charlie had beds of potato plants growing and harvesting year round and soup made from cabbages. Charlie's potatoes were also the major ingredient of the family favourite potato pancakes. Rationing of certain foods made them either expensive or hard to get so Lizzie would regularly bake a family filler, the Depression cake. Milk, butter, sugar and eggs were replaced with molasses and lard that were mixed with flour and some baking powder. A heavy but filling snack regularly alternated with cornbread that only required cornmeal, water and salt. The children were amazed that with one can of sardines or baked beans or even tinned corned beef their mother could create a family meal thinly spread on homemade bread. Other free foods included dandelion salad, a yellow flowering weed common in Sydney lawns and gardens.

Those who could not find enough food relied on soup kitchens run by municipal councils and charity organisations. Lizzie in her own way did what she could, helping out at the St Francis Catholic Church soup kitchen. Magazines published instructions and recipes for making bottled preserves to allow people to supplement the susso. Lizzie also helped out at her children's school serving students free soup and a slice of bread. The depression would, however, result in many children and young people suffering from malnutrition.

The early 1930s saw the boys growing closer to their father. In 1930 Harry aged ten and Francis twenty-two shared the excitement of watching the great span that was being built over the harbour. It was on Harry's birthday that the incredible feat of joining the two opposite sections of the archway began. Francis, who was training as an engineer, discussed every detail of this huge metal structure. He knew weights, heights, number of bolts, everything. The three eagerly awaited its completion.

Another growing passion that Francis and his father shared was sport. Francis was a typical Australian boy so Charlie tried to learn and support a range of, to him, strange and foreign games. He learnt the rules of cricket and slowly mastered the skills, though watching a game only proved interesting if Francis was playing. Charlie played rugby league with his son and enjoyed the physicality of the game. Neither gambled but both listened intently to racing broadcasts, cricket and football. The test series of 1930 had been played ball by ball through the radio and Don Bradman was becoming a household name.

Francis could quote the figures: "At twenty one he scored 974 runs, including four centuries in seven test averaging 139 runs. He also scored a world record of 334 runs in one innings." The boys would take turns pretending to be him as they played cricket with their friends in the street or on the vacant block behind their home. Dismay hit the house during the 1932 series when the English captain Douglas Jardine had his fast bowlers like Harold Larwood bowl at the batters' bodies. Listening to the broadcast the men became agitated when the English won the first two tests easily. All hell broke loose when in the third test at Adelaide the captain Bill Woodfull was struck on the cheek and collapsed. Wicket keeper Bert Oldfield's skull was fractured and "the Don" was also hit. The English were a dirty word in the street and caused actual physical fights between families. It would be years before both international and local tensions were eased.

Charlie would also take the boys and sometimes Margaret to the fights and as a special treat, without Lizzie knowing and with his children sworn to secrecy, they went to the races. This was due to the spectacle, a fact that newspaper reports and radio broadcasts had turned a horse and racing into a legend. One particular racehorse, Phar Lap, had become a national hero, winning thirty-seven out of fifty-one races. Though they did not see him race it didn't diminish the excitement of the day watching the bookies yelling out their prices, seeing the wealthy of Sydney dressed in their fine clothes, experiencing the excitement of the crowds as they cheered with renewed vigour at each race. The boys were sure that their uncle had placed bets but neither discussed this with him.

In March 1932 the big day arrived with Charlie, Francis, Margaret and Harry leaving from home very early as they knew that there would be thousands of people attending the opening ceremony of the new harbour bridge. It was Charlie's favourite politician who was to cut the ribbon, the premier of NSW and leader of the Labor Party, Jack Lang. Though Charlie was a strong unionist and Labor supporter he also respected the man and there was a picture of him on the mantlepiece. Lang was the most colourful and forceful politician of the time, a powerful and convincing speaker. His policies called for more public works to create employment and for the reduction in pay of only the high wage earners. Charlie naturally approved of his policies and was heard in discussions with friends to use the popular cry of the day, "Lang is right". He had got annoyed when he saw the anti-Lang campaign that was in the paper and upset when one of his friends showed him a note that had been put in pay packets by the boss.

"During the time Mr Lang has been Premier, the number of unemployed has increased by no less than sixty-four thousand. Money that should be available for the expansion of industry has been driven from the state. Confidence had been destroyed. Our credit has almost gone. The state has been brought near to bankruptcy. The people are being rapidly brought to ruin and despair. Clearly some new policy must be found. What should be done? Think it over."

Though they got to the bridge very early the crowds were huge and most of the children attending could not see anything. Francis and his father both lifted children onto their broad and strong shoulders and it was one of them who yelled out when they first saw the horsemen. As the premier was about to cut the ribbon a horseman rode up and cut it with a sabre, then all hell seemed to break loose. Fortunately the police arrested the rider otherwise many of Jack Lang's supporters including Charlie would have strung him up. It was one of the only times that his children heard him express himself violently. The ribbon joined once again, Jack had his go. The rest of the day was pleasant walking over the bridge and Charlie buying each of his children a large sweet that was shaped like the Harbour Bridge and another bridge model made of metal as a keepsake.

Charlie was disappointed later that year when Lang lost the election sixty-two seats to twenty-four. In the working class seats Lang was a hero and across the state Lang's party won nearly half the total vote.

'Those conservatives had the election rigged, there are seats with only a handful of people, it's unfair on the poor, the rich and wealthy landowners have too much power.'

Chapter 25

The shed

It was over two years after Irene's death before Charlie could bring himself to work on his ships in bottles. It had been something they had done together; Irene had the patience and fine motor skills to do the intricate work required. They spent hours designing and building and as they worked the two spoke only in Swedish, Irene constantly improving her language skills and reading texts her father would write. She loved poetry, writing in English then with her father's help translating to Swedish. On the wall stood a small bookshelf with about half a dozen books. These had belonged to Irene and included *My Brilliant Career* and *Some Everyday Folk and Dawn*, both written by Miles Franklin. Charlie got a shock when Irene had corrected his comment about his books. 'Her name was Stella Miles Franklin.' There was also *Up the Country*, a book written in 1928 by Brent of Bib Bin, a pseudonym used by Miles Franklin, sadly a present that Irene had been too ill to read.

On the shelf were kept games Irene played with Charlie. A Parker Brothers box containing the card game

Rook that used colours rather than the traditional suits, created for people with religious objections to the standard deck used for gambling. The board game Coppit, a variety of Parchisi, another box with Backgammon and one containing Checkers. Irene's favourite had been chess, preferring the traditional rules but having fun with Marseillais chess which allowed players to move twice per turn. Irene's books contained a copy of a book based on chess but not as they played it. It had been written by Edgar Rice Burroughs and was called *Chessmen of Mars*. In the book the game was called Jetan, played on an arena sized board with each taking of a piece being a duel to the death. Irene had read many of Burroughs' books, his *Tarzan of the Apes* series, and the science fantasy Martian series.

Another of Irene's Parkers games was Pegity, a sixteen by sixteen grid with a hole in the centre of each square where players took turn placing coloured pegs trying to get five in a row. The game also included printed patterns that younger children could copy to create patterns.

Harry was ten when he convinced his father to teach him the skill of creating these ornaments, with their trick of fitting a sailing ship through the narrow neck of a bottle. They started by drawing the ship in the size and shape, at first a single mast yacht then two and three mast ships. Small pieces of timber were chosen then carved and sanded into shape. The hull was made of layers, a keel and rudder added to the bottom layer and holes drilled on the top layer for sails to be added. Charlie was very particular about the colours used to paint the layers of the hull, insisting on authenticity. While Harry sanded and painted Charlie would cut two small wooden stands, curved on the base to be glued inside the bottle to form a base to hold the ship's hull. He drilled a tiny hole through the hull and base of the mast to allow for a thin piece of wire to act as a hinge, thus once the ship was placed into the bottle a long twine could be used to stand the mast, with its paper sail already attached, upright to be glued in place.

As they worked they listened to the radio, an Amalgamated Wireless Australia, AWA, Radiola 90. This was a six valve, all electric model in an upright cabinet. Charlie had purchased two, one for his shed, to listen to the sport and shows he liked and one for the house that Lizzie and the children could select their favourite broadcasts on. Charlie often listened to 2GB and found he liked a new presenter, Jack Davey. Davey had started as a singer but quickly began having his own talk and quiz shows. Each morning he enjoyed the *Hi ho everybody!* Breakfast show. Later, though not knowing many of the answers, Charlie would listen to his quiz show *That's What You Think* and Crazy Dave's evening program.

Near his father's workbench was the lawn mower that had been one of Harry's chores since he had turned ten. The current one, a push mower, made in Marrickville by Crowe was the Rex. It had been described as technically advanced, having ball bearings to allow reverse wheel motion, hardened steel blades, and grooved side wheels for extra traction and ground handling. But for Harry these blades were still powered by manual force, he still had to push and pull, the blades jamming if the grass was too wet or too thick. Harry had seen in a paper that an engine powered mower had been built by the Atco company in England in 1921 but was selling at seventy-five pounds. Even if available, they were well beyond the average family's budget with the 1920 average Australian factory workers income being around two hundred pounds a year.

For storage Charlie had taken the large meat safe out of the kitchen when they purchased an ice chest. The safe had a timber frame with two hinged doors made of the same metallic screen material that covered the external walls. It was free-standing with legs to keep it off the floor. It no longer had the cloth external layer that in the past was kept wet so any flow of air cooled the interior of the safe. It now held an array of children's' toys, Francis's old cricket bat and stumps, some balls in need of inflation, a box of old dolls, most awaiting repair, and two boxes of empty half gallon fruit jars, lids and clip springs. These jars were waiting to be filled with the fruit and vegetables grown in their own garden.

The back wall was lined in timber with hooks of all shapes and sizes holding suspended tools, an old pushbike frame and wheels, Charlie's old wet weather coats and both male and female gardening hats. One sat for years, a drooping broad brimmed straw hat trimmed with a wide sash of satin Bengaline and a cluster of artificial flowers on its crown. Charlie had bought it for Irene and each time he looked at it he allowed memories of happier times to replace some of his sadness.

Chapter 26

1931

Margaret stood in the back yard of her childhood home. She would remember the very moment, being there for ages floating, listening to the sounds of the city that had grown to engulf this once semirural block. She recalled hearing the tram rattle down to the Norton Street intersection and wished she was on it, anywhere but here. This was the only home she had known though her parents had taken her to see the houses in the inner city, Millers Point, Kent Street and Paddington where they used to live and where her older brothers and sisters had been born. Her parents were intensely proud that they owned this, their first and only home. It was on a large block and unlike the inner city was still spared the noise of busy road frontages and back lanes with rickety fences, rampant creepers, ramshackle sheds and the discarded excesses of daily existence.

 Once inside Margaret, then fourteen, joined the others and slowly walked past the open coffin. The white coffin lay on two low trestles and all the other furniture in the room was covered with white sheets. The almost rag doll like youth that lay there with a shiny penny on each once deep blue eye, was now a familiar sight. Here was her sister Esma, pale and distant in a white dress with a prayer book under her folded hands. The shock and terror of death was gone. In this atmosphere of musty smells, candle-lit darkness and tears, so many tears, she felt an acceptance. She was almost resigned to this being the hand of God that she had heard her mother say in her still strongly accented English. 'What God?' her father snapped back, his strong face filled with pain, a defeated and tormented soul.

'Goodbye, Essie,' she whispered softly.

It was her mother's wish that each of the family spend some time in the room alone with their departed sister. That short period of being scared to the point of paralysis remained as a torment in Margaret's mind for a very long time.

Upon returning to the main family group she looked around the large depressing lounge room draped in the trappings of sorrow and noted a marked contrast between the tall block-like family members from her father's Swedish side and the shorter stockier Irish relatives of her mother. The cultural context was also apparent. The Swedes stood statue-like, cold, motionless as in empathy with the departed, the Irish chatting, an unexpected family gathering a time to catch up, to talk of the wake, the celebration of the child's short life.

The Carlsson children had been brought up in the strong Catholic faith of their mother. Her father, though long since losing any faith he might have had, was from a

Lutheran background. He, at the church's request, had signed a document indicating that the children would be baptised and raised as Catholics. This was the small price he had to pay to be allowed to marry into a strong Catholic family.

Margaret's eyes were drawn to the sepia pictures on the wall.

'Such a proud family.'

She stopped, realising that though talking to herself it was loud enough that several of the mourners gave her side glances.

The next day Margaret sat in the church with Harry and listened to Father Donnet; she still shuddered to think about his words,

'How fortunate is your family to have another child called to Heaven by God to sit at his side.'

It was not surprising that neighbours and even family members used the word cursed when referring in private to the Carlssons.

The hearse, a solid black carriage with etched glass sides, stood outside their house. Late in the morning the cortège had moved slowly down the narrow street toward the station. The four black horses decked out in silver with black plumes on their heads strained as the large wheels creaked into motion. There was also a mourning coach with one horse and the family all in black walked solemnly behind.

Margaret remembered the solid sandstone of the mausoleum station. Its carved pillars and Roman design looked too impressive and beautiful to be wasted as a gathering point for grief ridden souls whose minds would be reflecting on the life of their lost ones.

They were but one of the mourning groups who joined the eight carriage train that carried coffins and family to final resting places. Once the large mourning parties boarded the train it moved away in billows of black smoke towards the Rookwood Cemetery. Here, at an equally impressive station building, the mass of bemoaning, wailing clusters of indistinct faces separated as each respective funeral wound its way to the allocated section of the large cemetery. Protestant here, Greek Orthodox there, Catholic down the hill, weren't all the decaying bodies in the coffins the same? Margaret couldn't understand this need for separation, especially now when souls were supposedly already in heaven or hell.

The long walk from the train, the lowering of the coffin, the frightful noise of heavy clods of clay being thrown in until the grave was filled, the pressure of her father's hand, the final realisation that she would never see Essie again, somehow hardened her view on many things. It was at these times she would hold tight to her other half, Harry.

The family plot, which her father had bought, contained spaces for ten. Her father had imagined that he and his wife would form the base with space for all his children to join them at their allotted time. How, not even in their worst nightmare, could they have imagined that his beloved children would lay stacked like boxes on shelves.

The priest's words were of no consolation to most of those who stood silently, all read the stone and asked why?

Esma had been born in 1915, the first of the Carlsson children born in the house they had purchased in Leichhardt. Unlike her older siblings she was baptised at St Fiacres Catholic Church in Catherine Street, Leichhardt. She attended the St Fiacres Primary school that dated back to 1888 and was run by the Sisters of St Joseph. She had none of the grace or beauty of her older sister Irene and far preferred climbing trees, playing cricket with the neighbourhood boys and when allowed going fishing with her brother Francis. Though she was sent for piano lessons at St Martha's Convent in Renwick Street, it was the nuns who recommended the lesson end. Despite regular rapping of a wooden rule over her fingers, Esma could not master the notes. She would squirm and complain, constantly asking how much time was left in the lesson. The nuns constantly corrected her about her posture. Sister Mercy, a joke, Esma thought, had even tied a stick to her back to keep it straight during lessons.

Esma was two when Margaret was born and five when an unexpected Harry arrived. She often felt the odd one out, overshadowed by her older and younger siblings. Francis and Irene spent most of their time together and seemed so grown up; Margaret and Harry did the same sharing secrets and whispering together. In a way this had made her competitive, always wanting to be seen as doing things better than the others. Esma was also more independent than the others, her focus turned to friendships rather than family. Whenever she could, she would get away visiting friends' houses, often getting in trouble for staying out too late or going too far away from home. Inwardly she would smile when her mother rebuked her; after all when this was happening she had the full attention of the family. She also got in trouble for constantly telling Margaret and Harry what they could or could not do. To her, their needs were always put before hers.

Because of the size of their family Esma had to share a room with Irene and Margaret. Charlie had enclosed a section of the side veranda and this had become the girls' bedroom. At the time there was limited understanding of how consumption spread. Esma and Margaret sharing was thought to brighten the life of their unwell daughter Irene and with her death in 1928 no one could have imagined the inevitable fatal link.

When Esma became too ill to remain at home, Charlie and Lizzie were forced to move her into the Queen Victoria Homes for Consumptives. This was a free private hospital for the care of patients suffering from tuberculosis located at Wentworth Falls in the Blue Mountains that had been opened in 1903. It was founded by John Goodlet, a Scottish timber merchant and philanthropist. He had established a sawmill and wharf in Erskine Street, a brickworks at Granville and a pottery at Surry Hills. He had been a company director for AMP, councillor at St Andrew's College and set up his first house for tuberculosis suffers in a hotel in Picton before his purpose-built facility was opened in Thirlmere in 1866.

In Victorian times climate prescriptions began to dominate the medical world. Because exposure to the bracing mountains climate of free air was desirable, the Blue Mountains was deemed ideal for consumption recovery. The Wentworth Falls building had been the retreat for Sir Kelso King, a prominent businessperson around 1890. After his wife died in 1900 King sold the property to the Committee of the Queen Victoria Diamond Jubilee Homes for Consumptives. Because of the spread and threat of this disease it was one of three sanatoria the committee developed in the Blue Mountains. The other two were Boddington Hospital, where Irene had been a patient and the R.T. Hall Home in Hazelbrook. All the homes were designed by George Sydney Jones the son of the leading expert on consumption at the time, Dr Phillip Sydney Jones.

In 1911 the Queen Victoria Sanatorium acquired state funding and became a hospital under the State Hospital Act. Summer and winter patients were housed in unheated, open-air chalets, bathed daily in cold water. Activities were encouraged. Patients could garden, play tennis, and indulge in bush walks in the countryside owned by the hospital. Expectorating on the ground was forbidden and Esma had to carry her own pocket sputum flask. Although the disease was highly infectious, family visits were encouraged, with Charlie and family members allowed to visit out in open spaces.

It was Charlie who visited every second weekend. Lizzie could not cope with seeing her daughter fading away. Their son-in-law Bill would drive him up in his Oldsmobile F29 convertible roadster, waiting for hours before driving Charlie home. At the end of the cold mountain winter Charlie was advised to take Esma home. She was now bedridden and her condition deteriorating. Again Bill drove Charlie to the sanatorium and helped him carry her out to the car. She was a shadow of her former self, coughing repeatedly. Margaret still shared a room with Esma, again the presumed benefits of companionship but this also resulted in Margaret developing symptoms. Fortunately, though she would have what she called a weak chest for the remainder of her life, the symptoms were mild and she recovered relatively quickly.

Chapter 27

Francis 1918–1934

Harry was only fourteen when his brother was injured. Comparing Carl and Francis was perhaps unfair as they were very different in all but the same magnificent crop of crisp, curly, jet-black hair. Unlike his older brother, Francis had no musical ability but loved swimming and was an excellent cricketer, playing for the Leichhardt Guild Cricket Club. Francis had been born at Millers Point but attended school at St Fiacres which only had nuns teaching the children. Thus at the age of twelve all boys were transferred to St Joseph's where they were taught by brothers. He had been an altar boy and right through his life seemed to be completely involved in church activities. He of all the family was the most compliant of Lizzie's children and worked with his mother, spending a great deal of his spare time helping the under privileged children in the local parish.

Francis left school at sixteen to become an apprentice to an engineering company. He only had one girlfriend, Colleen, who also was a member of the local church and from a strict Irish Catholic family. Her long flowing red hair and beautiful eyes had immediately captured Francis's heart. They were soul mates, not having to speak but still knowing exactly what the other was thinking. Constant companions right through their teens, Colleen was an automatic inclusion on all family outings and at all family parties. She went everywhere with him even keeping score at the local cricket matches. As cars were beyond the means of most young folk, pushbikes or public transport were all they could afford. Margaret could still remember the disapproval by both sets of parents when Colleen bought a pushbike to go around with Francis, dressed in shorts and an open necked shirt in summer, which was considered "not the right thing for a young lady to do".

Margaret was one of the few people who knew of their secret engagement. Colleen was only seventeen at the time and they knew her parents would not formally approve until she was twenty-one. Colleen's parents would not waver from this decree.

In 1929 and 1930 at the start of the Great Depression, Francis had been fortunate to keep his job but had to accept taking a wage cut or be replaced by third or fourth year apprentices. He had become a journeyman in 1930 and remained with the foundry until it closed in 1931. Though he could not find another position he was not eligible for the government dole as this was only available to people where no other member of the family had a job, and his father was employed.

Francis and Colleen did become formally engaged in 1931, setting a date of marriage in June 1935. A long engagement in their minds but as Francis had no job, car or home, it was the date that Colleen's parents had agreed to as they would be paying for the wedding.

Francis was always aware of his responsibilities and demonstrated persistence and determination. As a local junior cricket coach he tackled all obstacles in small steps, believed in celebrating all team achievements but most of all he encouraged his team to work towards constant improvement while still having fun. Francis applied this to his own life as well.

Francis was a hard worker and determined that the Depression would not beat him. He started to take on any part-time work he could find and then decided to try an egg and butter run using his pushbike with a large basket set on a frame over the front wheel. It was hard work having to ride to Lidcombe to collect a half case of eggs then to the Sydney Co-op for butter. Initially he rode around the streets calling out but quickly developed a steady list of permanent clients. His initiative had paid off but as the Depression dragged on, many of his customers were finding it more difficult to keep up their payment and Francis, soft-hearted like his father, allowed some of the needier ones to slip further into debt which made it more difficult for him as he had to pay cash at the depots.

At the beginning of 1934 things were looking a little brighter and it seemed that the foundry was in the process of re-starting. Both he and Colleen were excited at the prospect of their wedding getting closer and with the money they had saved the possibility of their own place to live.

Though for most families the Depression had been years of turmoil and hardship, for the Carlssons it had been five years of relative peace. The family had been able to afford to still have outings and family holidays and they were looking forward to a June wedding.

After a happy Saturday outing to the Botanic Gardens, Sunday afternoon following mass and youth group commitments, Francis, Colleen and Harry headed off to a charity cricket match being held at Clifton Garden at the end of the seasons. There were two games in progress on the same oval when Francis, fielding in the outfield, was struck behind the ear by a ball hit from the other pitch. He was rushed to Manly Hospital, unconscious. The wound was stitched and Francis remained in hospital for a week but when he arrived home it was obvious that something was wrong.

The medical finding was, due to the blow on the head, a small blood vessel had been ruptured causing a blood clot that brought on partial paralysis. Francis was confined to bed, his beloved Colleen constantly by his side. The prognosis was bleak and the atmosphere of the house reflected it. Everything was silent; meals were at a whisper, the long gaunt faces showing the stress. Francis slipped in and out of coma, complained of terrible headaches and had lost all use of his right arm and leg.

Harry found it the hardest to accept the inevitable. He was determined to keep Francis's small business going so each day after he returned home from his own job he was out on Francis's bike into the darkness making deliveries. It was during this time that Harry learnt a lot about human nature. Francis had kept a book that showed all customers, their orders and payments made. Though most were good, many just left notes out with their orders and no money; other argued about payment indicating they had paid but Francis had not recorded it. After a few days he found that if he called around when they were not expecting him he could see these women, many friends of his mother, talking to neighbours, suddenly break the conversation and hurry inside. Even though he knew they were there his knocking went unanswered.

As a kid, Harry believed himself to be tough but was in tears when he had to face his brother with not enough cash to carry on his business. He was devastated by the disappointment in his brother's ailing eyes. These good church people, many supposed to be friends, had exploited the current circumstances. Charlie put an end to this sometimes embarrassing situation by having accounts made out for all outstanding debts and Harry delivered them via letter boxes. Harry had no idea how many, if any, of these people paid but the matter was never mentioned in their home again.

Harry moved into his brother's room both to give his sister privacy but also to be near his brother who he loved and admired. Colleen would still sit every day with Francis but the stress was telling on her and her parents walked her home each evening to have a break.

Now not able to talk and also recognising people less and less, Francis woke Harry in the night making a noise and pointing at the disused fireplace.

'What is it, Francis?'

Harry imagined he was hallucinating.

'There's no fire, we're all right.'

Francis again slumped into silence. The next morning, the same cry was repeated, the waving more frantic as if to convey a message. Harry walked in the direction his brother pointed. When he reached the fireplace Francis's arm slightly moved, desperately urging Harry to one side. Harry reached up into the chimney and on a ledge he could feel a rectangular shape. He moved further forward and could grasp the small but heavy metal box which he took out of its hiding place, putting it on the drawer next to Francis's bed.

'What is it, Francis?'

Harry opened the lid,

'Hell, what's this!'

He reached into the box and took out the roll of notes and could see a large amount of coins that had produced the box's weight. This had been Francis's secret hiding place, his savings for his and Colleen's future. As Harry turned to share his findings he noticed that Francis now lay still. He stepped towards him and lifted his outstretched arm that lay in the direction of the floor; he was at peace and Harry left the room to get his father.

The coffin was set up in his room and hundreds of his friends came to pay their respects before the funeral the next day. Harry sat with Margaret watching the procession and noting that none of the people who owed Francis money came to the house.

The following day at the church Harry surveyed the mourners all dressed in black. Amongst them were some of the people who had closed their doors on him and lied about paying their bill, robbing Francis, but here they were to watch his family grieve. To the shock of all assembled, Harry in a tearful and angry outburst let fly verbally accusing and abusing all, but naming some specifically, with language that was aggressive and foul. Lizzie's expression was one of embarrassment rather than shock.

Charlie contained his wife and it was Colleen who understood and quickly came to Harry's assistance, taking him out of the church and home. They didn't go to the cemetery and that evening when the family returned, the house was filled with his mother's yelling and aggression rather than grief. Whatever relationship Harry had previously experienced with his mother it was shattered by her reaction. All he could see was that her public standing in the community, made up of people who had lied and stolen, was more important than her family, their feelings and needs.

He walked out of the house, intent on never speaking to her again. It was his sister Margaret who followed him out. Of all the family she had been the one who had been able to calm him down and talk sense into him. As the youngest two, they were the ones who seemed to have inherited their mother's short fuse. Naturally this meant that they were the ones who challenged their mother, questioning her instructions and rules.

It took Harry hours but he walked from Leichhardt to his Uncle Anders' cottage in Marine Parade, Watsons Bay. Anders would listen, he always did. Charlie left the boy with his brother for nearly a week before heading there on the pretext of a day's fishing. Anders had contacted them so they knew where he was but Charlie was dealing with a two sided see-saw, getting Harry home and convincing Lizzie that the boy was right. Not the way he had handled it, but right to be upset and angry. Though Charlie had shielded Lizzie from the egg run dilemma he knew he had to explain what had gone on with Francis, the money, Harry's efforts to keep his brother's business going, what neighbours and supposed friends had done. He also knew this was a risk; Lizzie could forgive her son but she might also take on the cause, adding more conflict to neighbourhood tensions.

With the death of Esma in 1931 being followed by the loss of her son just over two years later, and now this conflict with Harry and her supposed friends, Lizzie just listened, walked into their bedroom, closed the door and cried. She had often suffered from migraines, but in the past Charlie had picked her up, carried her into their bedroom, put brown paper soaked in vinegar on her forehead and left her alone in the darkness. Lizzie was also prone to fainting spells but her children often thought this was just an escape.

Chapter 28

1935

Charlie was aware that his son Carl had taken leave from the navy and was working in Western Australia. He had used his savings to purchase a pearling boat. Carl had been reasonably successful till the 29th of March when a cyclone had struck the pearling fleet off the coast at Broome. This brought back chilling memories for Charlie as his own shipwreck had been off the Western Australian coast. Carl did not dive himself as this required the skill called free diving, a technique where a diver in shallow water descends to the bottom, collects what they can, and surfaces on a single breath. For deeper water and a longer time undersea, Carl's boat also carried an underwater helmet and canvas diving suit that connected air hoses with a pump on the boat. Though allowing divers to descend to a depth of thirty-six metres, there were constant threats of shark attacks as well as decompression sickness called the bends.

The pearl hunters recovered pearls from wild molluscs, usually oysters and mussels, in the sea. It was not a new industry, having started in Australia in the 1850s, but by the early 1900s Broome had become the focal point of the industry. The four hundred or so luggers operating out of Roebuck Bay employed over 3500 people. The area had attracted a large number of Europeans, South Sea Islanders and Asians who came for adventure, the promise of work and the chance to make their fortune. Carl, like most of the "Pearling Masters" were people who owned boats, mainly Europeans. Their mixed race crews did the dangerous work. Carl mainly employed Japanese divers and the ones on his boat were indentured labour, working for little money in order to repay a debt, their transport to Australia.

The unnamed cyclone of 1935 had resulted in the loss of twenty-one pearling luggers and the death of a hundred and forty-one men, mainly pearlers. The fleet had been near Lacepede Islands off the Kimberly coast, about 120 kilometres north of Broome when the storm struck. It was not the first pearling disaster due to a cyclone; in 1887, 1910 then 1935, a total of over eighty luggers had been lost and three hundred crew. However, in 1935 other winds of change were brewing with the threat of Japanese expansion. When Japan attacked Pearl Harbour on the 7th of December 1941, the pearling fleet was ordered south to Fremantle to prevent the luggers falling into enemy hands. Many didn't make it but those that did were burnt on the beach; the pearling industry was over.

Following the loss of his lugger Carl saw no option but to re-join the navy. He had travelled to Sydney to see his parents and siblings but only spent a few days. The anguish of lost siblings made the visit unbearable thus much of his time was spent at the King Cross clubs, gambling and drinking, his own form of escaping from reality.

He did have some family time with Margaret and Harry. In October a new amusement park had opened in Sydney called Luna Park. It was located on the northern shore of the harbour in the suburb of Lavender Bay almost under the northern approach to the Sydney Harbour Bridge that had opened three years earlier. It was not the first as in 1912 a Luna Park had been opened in St Kilda, Melbourne and in 1930 another in Glenelg, South Australia. Both of these had been based on the success of the first Luna Park which opened on Coney Island, New York in 1903. The Sydney park's rides had previously been located at the Glenelg Park but because of financial difficulties had been dismantled and moved to the Sydney site.

With its opening, long queues waited in front of the park's notable giant face. Most wanted to rush in to be one of the first on the Big Dipper, the park's rickety roller coaster. The park was described as offering thrill-giving mechanical contrivances all embellished with fantastic designs or grotesqueries in vivid colours. Just inside the entrance was an enormous spider, under which were cars on a circular track, known as the tumble bug. They rode on the ghost train and the river cave, in boats on a stream of water through scenic and model effects. As a fifteen-year-old Harry's favourite was the dodgem cars, deliberately crashing into his brother. This was one of the few fond memories that Margaret and Harry had of their older brother. It would be a further four years before the three would again join in a convivial outing.

Not long after Carl left again the news was full of the death of Sir Charles Kingsford Smith. Smithy, as he was referred to, was a dare devil and folk hero who had made the first transpacific flight from the United States to Australia in 1928 in a Fokker monoplane called the Southern Cross. He had also made the first non-stop crossing of the Australian mainland and the first flight between Australia and New Zealand. In 1929 with friend and partner Charles Ulm they established the Australian National Airways carrying passengers, mail and freight between Sydney, Brisbane and Melbourne. Not the first as in 1920 the Queensland and Northern Territory Service, QANTAS, had become Australia's first airline. Sadly, while flying his plane the Lady Southern Cross from Allahabad in India to Singapore as part of an attempt to break the England to Australia speed record, they hit a storm over the Andaman Sea, their bodies never found.

Harry, like so many of his generation, was inspired by these early pioneers. In 1937 he was fascinated to read Kingsford Smith's autobiography which became a bestseller.

He had also read what articles he could find about a man called Reverend John Flynn. In 1928 Flynn had formed the Aerial Medical Service based in Cloncurry, Queensland and by 1934 the service had bases in Port

Headland, Kalgoorlie, Broken Hill, Alice Springs, Meekatharra, Charters Towers and Charleville. In 1937 Dr Jean White was to become the first female flying doctor in the world.

Harry had a map of Australia on his wall and marked in the places, amazed at their remoteness and distances. He remembered from school about the opening up of this vast continent and recalled the feat as far back as 1872 of a 3200 kilometre telegraph line that joined Darwin and Port Augusta in South Australia being completed. With the limited technology of the time, repeater stations had to be built, each three hundred kilometres along the line. In 1936 there had even been a submarine communications cable between Victoria and Tasmania.

The thought of flying, even becoming a pilot, had a certain fascination, but all aspects of air travel were not encouraging. In May the giant airship the Hindenburg had exploded in a ball of flames while attempting a landing in New Jersey. The airship had already made ten safe crossings of the Atlantic Ocean between Germany and the United States. There had been concerns about a balloon filled with highly flammable hydrogen gas but it had been presumed safe.

For Margaret, Harry and their friends, another fad that had swept the country was a new board game called Monopoly. It had been released in the US mid-1936 and had now become an essential in most Australian homes. Margaret had helped unpack the hundreds of boxes that her workplace sold during the Christmas rush. She was sure it must have been the most demanded gift of that year.

Chapter 29

The old country, 1936

Following the death of Francis, Charlie had retreated into a permanent state of depression and isolation. His enthusiasm for life was gone and with it his appetite. Carl had not been heard from for over two years and Harry had informed them he was planning on spending some time visiting the Central Coast and would be taking his nephew Keith with him. Keith had become like another son to Charlie and he was immensely proud of his outstanding achievements at school. He had initially resented Lizzie's decision to send Keith as a boarder to St Joseph's College as the money his father Bill sent did not cover the expenses and he missed having the boy around. However, the outcomes had been pleasing; Keith was a fine young man with prospects, who could ask for more.

With family encouragement the decision was made that Lizzie needed a break from the sadness of current life and should go and see the old country.

'It will give you a new lease on life, help you move on.'

This was the type of persistent comments coming mainly from Lizzie's sisters. Normally she would have ignored them, told them to mind their business, but she was desperately worried about how Charlie was acting and decided that a cruise might be the answer.

Lizzie's family thought they should fly. The flying boat from Sydney to London only took ten days, with only nine overnight stops and twenty-four other landings. There was a thrice weekly service which Qantas Empire Airways advertised as: "Effortless speed, solid comfort and unforgettable scenic beauty without the least vestige of a thrill".

It sounded good till the price was mentioned, two hundred pounds each way.

'No,' a shocked Lizzie protested, 'the round trip from Sydney to London by ship is only eighty-six pounds, that's more than enough.'

There were several options; some sailed by the Cape of Good Hope and though the cheapest, the Atlantic Ocean could be very rough. Others chose to cross the Pacific to California and went by train to New York and boarded a Cunard liner for the last leg, but the most popular route which they also took was via the Suez Canal. They sailed tourist class on the P&O liner *Strathaird* via Singapore, Colombo, the Suez then Naples and on to London, the trip taking thirty-four days.

Lizzie's letters to her sister reflected her disposition as various elements of the trip evolved.

Singapore was very civilised, a British colony, hot but a pleasant change from the rocking of the ship. We both had a touch of seasickness for the first few days but are fine now. Some lovely people though Charlie is keeping very much to himself, his face still looks drawn and tired. He had a tour of the ship which he found fascinating and one of the officers seeks him out to talk sailing ships and exotic ports, he is always much brighter after one of their discussions. I'm glad we came. There are three women to every man on the ship. The only age where men outnumber women are in the under ten and over sixty groups. During our stay our guide pointed out the large guns being installed as part of the Singapore defence system. We were told the guns were originally destined for the cruiser Furious. *We also saw a new naval base being built, apparently as a deterrent to the increasingly ambitious Japanese Empire.*

She was less flattering about Colombo.

My first real foreign port. Charlie has been here before but says it is totally different. We hired a car with a nice native driver who took us around. We wouldn't have done it ourselves but another couple from Melbourne who sit at our table for meals insisted so we went along. I didn't enjoy the native people constantly wanting to sell you goods. I would prefer it if you could just purchase what you wanted and then they would go away. Very hot and sticky, I'm looking forward to the cooler climate in Europe. Our driver told us that there had been a drought which had caused a shortage of rice, the people's staple food. He also expressed some concern for the future as the Marxist Lanka Sama Samaja Party had developed and is demanding independence. Though the younger ones make good use of the ship's deck games I'm playing bridge each afternoon, and spending my mornings reading. The food had been really excellent, it might have been nice to experience first class but this is more than suitable. Charlie is excited about going through the Suez Canal, he is really looking forward to seeing how they have cut the canal through the desert reducing travel time to England by weeks. The canal wasn't here when he was sailing so it will be another new experience. There were lots of British Army officers and their families that joined the ship in Colombo. It is mainly the lower ranking officers travelling tourist class and some of their wives have made their displeasure very clear. Their stories of life in Sri Lanka and India sound simply wonderful. Imagine having lots of house servants. I feel a lot of these ladies have never done a day's work in their lives.

Today we entered the Suez Canal, an artificial sea-level waterway on over 100 miles connecting the Red Sea with the Mediterranean Sea. I'm not sure what I expected but all I could see was sand. We sailed in at the city of Suez, a single lane waterway but ships could pass in a lake called The Bitter Lake. Charlie has spent hours on the deck just watching the sand dunes and scattered settlement.

Lizzie could not understand why they needed to go via Naples; it seemed out of the way.

Naples is a very shabby city and no one could speak English. I expected lovely old Roman buildings but everything is in need of a good paint, there seem to be clothes hanging on lines from every window and the rubbish, it's just deposited in the streets. I think this to be a filthy place and will be glad to be on our way again.

Today arrived at Gibraltar, a large rock with a busy British naval base at its base. A considerable number of our fellow travellers, mostly those in the military, disembarked this morning. After lunch on the ship we walked into the township passing through a Moorish defence wall to Casemates Square with an ached gateway built into a stone wall. The buildings are a mix of Spanish and British, saw a red mail box and a very English looking policeman. The city hall for the Gibraltar Colonial Authority was a spectacular building, a three-storey pink mansion that used to be a private house. Opposite it stood an even more impressive building, a four-storey colonnaded Georgian structure that turned out to be the fire brigade centre. We were surprised that most people seem to be speaking Spanish but you could tell the English, they seemed neater and certainly wore superior footwear. While having afternoon tea in a nice café we spoke to some very English sounding locals who told us the Spaniards filled an important role, the fishmongers, hawkers, grocers and barbers, all the menial positions. We had been told to be careful of the Monos which turned out to be the local name for the Barbary apes that lived on the rock. We had been told that a legend stated that as long as Gibraltar

Barbary macaques existed on Gibraltar, the territory would remain under British rule. We were taken to the Queen's Gate, part of the city's fortifications, where a large troop of apes lived. Some sounded aggressive while others jumped on people trying to get, I presume, food from their bags. Charlie joked it would be the British naval fleet rather than the apes who would assure control. I sent some postcards but refused to purchase those of smelly apes rather selecting ones showing the Royal Naval Hospital, an imposing three-storey building set high on the rock. I thought it would mean more to people as it was the hospital where many Australian, British and New Zealand wounded were taken off hospital ships during the World War One conflict at Gallipoli.

By comparison to especially Naples, arriving in England was such a relief. They could understand what people were saying, the place names made sense, and the food, good solid roasts, meat and vegetables.

The card Lizzie sent from Belfast had a drawing of the London Tower Bridge.

The English parks and countryside were so green and indescribably lush. Every second person we spoke to in London seemed to be from Australia. I'm sure half the country is over here. We only had two days in the city before we continued our journey by train then ferry to Belfast. Ireland somehow looks so much drabber, the colours less vibrant and the conditions seem so much poorer. I'm not surprised or disappointed, it's just different but the people are so friendly and welcoming.

The news in England wasn't good. There is talk of war, and when we were in London there were bombers and spitfires racing through the skies, getting ready for what many people feel is inevitable. The German leader named Hitler had his troops enter the Rhineland, which the papers say had been declared a demilitarised zone according to the Treaty of Versailles. London is drenched with propaganda, appeals for all types of things and lots of emergency instructions. We were even offered gas masks but didn't take them. I think Australia to be a paradise, its isolation protecting it from the horrors of the world. Nothing like that here in Ireland, though I'm not sure which side the Irish would support, they are so anti English. It is very cold and Charlie seems to have caught a bad chill. Tomorrow will be our first contact with relatives, how very exciting.

Her next letter carried an increasing air of concern.

Charlie is still unwell, the cold and damp conditions seemed to have increased his melancholy. Though my cousin Colin and his family want to take us places, most days Charlie excuses himself, indicating that he doesn't want the others to catch his ills, I'm having a wonderful time, met so many people and have lots of photographs to show you when we return. Only two weeks now and we head back to England. Travel has proven a bit of a problem as there has been a seventeen day bus strike and the army has intervened providing lorries for transport. The Church here is also very vocal. The Bishop of Galway has recently denounced immodest dress and vulgar films. Though I agree with this I don't think he should forbid Catholics from being members of the Irish Republican Army and Communist organisation, these are just people wanting greater freedoms, how can he call that a mortal sin?

Charlie spent most of the trip home in their cabin. He missed most meals and was only taking liquids by the time they reached Sydney.

With failing health, pneumonia had set in and Charlie showed no will to fight it. He refused to go to hospital or take any medicine; he had given up. This Lizzie would not accept. She badgered him constantly so rather than fighting he began to follow her instruction, more to get her off his back than anything else.

Chapter 30

1938

On an incredibly stinking hot February Sunday Harry, Margaret and her friends, Monica and Constance, decided to spend the day at the beach. They tossed up between Manly and Bondi but decided on the latter. There turned out to be thousands who had the same idea. The mood was festive as Sydney had recently celebrated its sesquicentenary with a grand parade called the Australian March to Nationhood. The day before their outing, Saturday the 5th of February 1938, the first Empire Games to be held in Australia had opened at the Sydney Cricket Ground. For this reason the beach was far more crowded than usual, later estimated at 35,000, and the ethnic diversity much greater. Though the weather was clear there was a large swell hitting the coast. The red and yellow striped flags indicating a safe swimming area were positioned almost directly opposite the Bondi Pavilion about 80 yards apart.

As the tide moved out, more and more people ventured out to the sandbar that ran parallel to the beach. Though the girls remained on the beach preferring to sunbake, Harry enjoyed the pounding waves, body surfing between the hundreds of other bobbing objects. He could hear the beach inspectors busily blowing their whistles, frantically waving to move people into a safer area. He was fine, he was a strong swimmer and felt the conditions were safe. He could see members of the Bondi Surf Bathers' Life Saving Club gathering for a surf race and watched boat crews dropping buoys to mark out a course for a race.

It was just on three o'clock when three large waves rolled in, washing away the sandbank. Suddenly the water was filled with people struggling to make it back to shore. The girls had grabbed their towels and run for safety as each wave surged high up the beach, not receding before the next surge. When the lull in the waves did eventuate, the massive backwash was phenomenal. Swimmers were swept out to sea.

On the beach there was a stunned but short-lived silence. Margaret scanned the water for her brother. Panic dominated the scene as the life savers sprang into action manning their surf reels, with beltmen wearing a belt with line attached diving into the swirling water to help those in danger. Their job had been made much harder as the unskilled crowd on the beach rushed to help. The beltmen found themselves swamped by swimmers, some who had to be pushed away to get to others in more danger.

Margaret could see that the surf boat was still out beyond the waves seemingly unaware of the drama. She counted over a hundred swimmers being brought to the beach with about sixty of them appearing unconscious. At one stage she saw about twenty people strewn across the beach being given resuscitation treatment by life savers. Eventually she spotted Harry; he was carrying a young girl from the surf, then without hesitation ran back into the water to help others. Panic had swept relatives and friends on the beach but the hastily summoned local police could not cope and had to call for reinforcement. The surf clubhouse took on the appearance of a hospital emergency ward. Margaret estimated it took about thirty minutes to clear the water. Given the scale of the disaster, it seemed incredible that only five people drowned. Margaret was proud of Harry; there were probably many heroes on the day that would be labelled Black Sunday but his bravery would remain unrecognised, the fear that their mother would find out about the danger they had been in.

There was also a concern that Lizzie would attempt to stop them going to the Empire Games events for which they had purchased tickets. Harry had been the driving force behind them attending. His interest dated back to his school days of 1930 when his teacher asked her students to do an assignment on the first Empire Games. The 1930 British Empire Games were the inaugural version of what became known as the Commonwealth Games, and were held in Hamilton, Ontario, Canada from the 16th to 23rd of August 1930. The games were organised by the *Hamilton Spectator*'s sportswriter Bobby Robinson after he attended the 1928 Summer Olympics in Amsterdam as manager of the Canadian track and field team and was inspired to create a similar event for the British Empire.

After campaigning for the idea among contacts he met at the Olympics, he was asked to organise the first British Empire Games in Hamilton.

There were eleven teams that participated: Australia, Bermuda, British Guiana, Canada, England, Ireland, Newfoundland, New Zealand, Scotland, South Africa and Wales. Men would compete in athletics, boxing, lawn bowls, rowing, swimming and wrestling. Women competed only in aquatic events, swimming and diving.

Harry had been required to draw a map of the world and mark on the participating countries, then select three to write some interesting facts about. Harry got a large sheet of brown paper and borrowed an atlas from his Uncle Anders. Before he could get started Charlie and Anders both decided to help. Between them they had visited most of these countries and were experienced with maps and charts. Harry was forced to first accurately measure and mark on major lines of latitude and longitude as that made marking in the continents much easier.

He loved this time with the men. As he drew in a country they would describe what they had seen there, the cargos their ships had collected and swapped life experiences. There were several "don't tell your mother but" moments, anecdotes, some boasting and lots of one-up-man-ship. When it came to selecting the three countries, again Harry got no say. Charlie indicated that Lizzie would not forgive Harry if he did not include her precious Ireland. Anders initially suggested his wife's homeland, Scotland, but they thought it was too much like

Ireland and settled on Bermuda, a tropical land where he talked about his first love. The third was to be South Africa. Both men had sailed around the Cape of Good Hope and spent time in Cape Town as goods and passengers were unloaded and new cargo sought.

By the time the second games were held in 1934, Harry was already leaving school for an apprenticeship. The 1934 British Empire Games were held in England, from the 4th to 11th of August 1934. The host city was London, with the main venue at Wembley Park. Seventeen national teams took part, including the Irish Free State (the only Games that they participated in before becoming the country of Ireland in 1937, though at the 1930 Games, an all-Ireland had team competed). The 1934 Games had been originally awarded to Johannesburg, South Africa, but the change of venue to London was made due to concerns regarding the treatment of black and Asian athletes by South African officials and fans.

Six sports were featured for men: athletics in White City Stadium; boxing, wrestling, and aquatics (swimming and diving) in the Empire Pool and Arena, Wembley; cycling and lawn bowls. For women athletics consisting of running, hurdles, high and long jump and javelin, was included with swimming and diving. Harry visualised being there but had to settle for the radio broadcasts on the Australian Broadcasting Corporation that had been established by the Lyons government in 1932. Besides the original eleven nations Hong Kong, India, Jamaica,

Northern Ireland, Southern Rhodesia and Trinidad and Tobago took part.

They had already been among the 36,000 spectators who had watched the opening of the 1938 games at the Sydney Cricket grounds on the Saturday. They had heard speeches and watched as 2000 pigeons were released. Within ten minutes of the completion of the ceremony competition commenced. They were to see the men's 100 yards heats and all three rounds of the women's 100 yards won by Australia's Decima Norman who had the nicknames of The White Streak, Dashing Dessie and The Flying Handful. With the rest of the crowd they jeered the starter when the Australian runner Thelma Peakes was disqualified for breaking at the start, though she had been disrupted by the javelin event taking place nearby. They watched as a Kiwi, Cecil Matthews, won the three-mile event and the final event of the day, the 440 yards hurdles won by Canadian John Loaring. The two-hour track and field program concluded at five p.m.

Feeling lucky with their Bondi escape behind them, remaining a secret, the four adventurers found themselves in trouble again just over a week later when they boarded the Sydney ferry the *Rodney*, for a cruise on the harbour to farewell a visiting US Navy cruiser, *USS Louisville*. They had paid a shilling each to see off the American cruiser. The new privately owned ferry, only built the year before, was licensed to carry two hundred and eleven passengers and on the 13th February was fully loaded. Margaret's friend Constance had become very close to one of the young sailors. The ship was one of seven warships in Sydney for the sesquicentenary of the arrival of the First Fleet at Sydney Cove. The *Louisville* had left her berth at Woolloomooloo with bands playing and onlookers cheering. The ship's six hundred uniformed sailors lined the decks. As the ferry drew alongside the Louisville, between Garden Island and Bradleys Head, the four friends, with most of the excited passengers, rushed upstairs to the portside of the ferry, giving it a dangerous list. As they were now in the ship's wash the ferry began to capsize, passengers spilling into the water, the ferry then rolling over, sinking in fifteen metres of water. Passengers on the upper deck near Harry and Margaret grabbed at floating seats and Harry helped his three companions stay afloat. Several of their friends who had remained on the lower deck and had not been able to break windows to escape were taken down to the bottom with the ferry.

The Manly ferry *Barrenjoey* and about twenty other boats who were nearby came to assist. Sailors from the *Louisville* dove in to help and the cruiser lowered four lifeboats and two motor launches to help in the rescue. Some survivors were taken on board the *Louisville* to the ship's hospital, others hauled onto other boats and brought ashore at the Man O'War Steps. Harry, Margaret and her friends had been taken aboard a large motor cruiser, the *Celere*. Though they objected they were transported to St Vincent Hospital and this time there was no hiding the drama from Lizzie. However, it turned out to be Charlie who felt the greatest impact of the news.

With the loss of his son Francis in 1934 and four daughters—Martina in 1901, Irene in 1928, Esma in 1931 and Maria in 1932—the ability to comprehend what might have been the outcome of the sinking of the *Rodney* was beyond him. The thought of the loss of Margaret and Harry constantly played on his mind. Having already become reclusive this just made it worse. His level of extreme anxiety and nervousness was leading to a greater fear of social contact and relationships. He avoided activities that involved being with others.

Harry tried to get his father to come fishing with him, to visit Anders at Watson Bay, but he repeatedly refused. Charlie had always enjoyed watching rugby league and his precious Balmain Tigers, but now wouldn't go to matches and when Harry tried to show him articles in the paper about the matches, just walked away. Harry was becoming distressed by this disinterest. Charlie in the past would dissect the games and talk about the great years when his club won the 1915, 1916, 1917, 1919, 1920 and 1924 premierships. In his shed Charlie had a jumper that Anders had given him, with its distinctive black and gold colours of the original 1908 thin strip jersey. Charlie also knew the team by The Watersiders, which was how many journalists referred to them and people who lived in the Leichhardt area. Harry and Margaret remembered their father taking them and Francis to home games at Birchgrove Oval and then for a short time at Wentworth Park, then Drummoyne Oval and from 1934 Leichhardt Oval.

Towards the end of the year Margaret and Harry constantly bickered with their mother who had decided Charlie could no longer live at home. Between them they felt that adequate care was being provided but both were at work during the day so Lizzie was left alone with Charlie. One evening on returning home they found their father gone, taken during the day to Lidcombe State Hospital for the aged in Joseph Street, Lidcombe. The concept was good as inmates assisted staff with farming activities, with vegetable gardens, a dairy herd and bakery, but for Charlie now frail and semi-bedridden, his outside activity consisted of sitting in one of the many armchairs on a cement veranda. Margaret and Harry visited when they could; Lizzie did not.

As the year ended the temperatures rose. Days were hot, records broken as the eastern capital experienced a series of days in the high forties Celsius. In January the fires started, first in Victoria and spreading north and west. The death toll rose quickly and at Matlock Forest fifteen men died at one timber mill. Whole towns like Omeo in the Victorian high country were lost and the damage to houses, property and timber ran into millions of pounds, and thousands of cattle were burnt alive.

For Margaret and Harry, June 1938 was a magical time in the sense that they had the opportunity to watch Walt Disney's *Snow White and the Seven Dwarfs*. The feature length animated musical fantasy film had required two million drawings and three years of work to develop. The comical Happy, Sleepy, Bashful, Sneezy, Grumpy,

Dopey and Doc had taken everyone's heart. Harry realised he related to the character Bashful, it was him to a tee. Margaret thought Happy reflected her nature but Harry considered Grumpy as a better match. Very soon they were singing along with *Whistle While You Work* and *Hi Ho, It's Off to Work We Go*. Margaret preferred *Some Day My Prince Will Come*; deep down that's the way she really felt. Though they felt sure it had been developed as a children's film, at nearly eighteen Harry was amazed how much he enjoyed and was moved by this epic story of love and friendship.

Chapter 31

Goodbye to a gentle man — July 1939

The good times should become comforting memories, but for the Carlssons memories of happy times could not outweigh grief. The pain of each loss felt overwhelming. Charlie experienced a range of difficult and unexpected emotions. Really he was in shock, an ideal life of the 1920s had been shattered. He felt anger, disbelief and profound sadness. Charlie was also surprised that he felt guilt. There was nothing he could have done to change reality but felt he should have. He was numb; his mind wanted to deny his losses but the reality of the funerals and having to support those around him forced him to face things as they actually existed. His grief also affected him physically. He struggled to sleep, eat and even think straight. Coping with the loss of those you love is one of life's biggest challenges. It is like a roller coaster full of highs and lows. His insomnia and nausea were a constant challenge; he suffered from weight loss and severe fatigue.

As he deteriorated Charlie was moved from the Lidcombe facility to the Liverpool State Hospital, an asylum that was originally established by the Sydney

Benevolent Society as a home for the destitute and infirm. Charlie died a lonely man, loved by many but shattered by life's experiences.

The service was held in a chapel at the crematorium and Margaret was pleased to see the level of turnout. Some old familiar faces of families her father had helped during the Depression, of children now grown that he had mended bikes and made toys for, of men who had worked with him on the docks and for whom he had fought to protect their jobs during those long hard years of the early 1930s. In the eyes of this gathering he was a great man; most knew little of his personal turmoil and grief. There was a genuine outpouring of loss and although there was a request for no wreaths or flowers their home was flooded with deliveries. Throughout the service Lizzie was cold and distant. Whether still keeping up appearances, playing the lady at the centre of this large stage, or in deep shock Margaret could not tell, as neither she, nor any other member of the family could really read Lizzie's emotions or motivations.

When Charlie died the family requested permission to bury the ashes at the family plot in Rookwood Cemetery. It was only right he should be with his children but the request was denied, it being a consecrated Catholic section of the cemetery. Thus late one afternoon just before closing time Margaret and Harry quietly spread the ashes over the double plot with its large white marble cross. There could be no plaque, it would have been taken down anyway, but he was now with them for eternity. For Harry who had long since lost his childhood faith, this he thought was a good reason for his father holding onto his Lutheran faith. It wasn't God who didn't want him with his family, just the bureaucracy of the Roman church.

Harry went back two weeks later with a timber plaque that he had carved and engraved himself. He moved aside some of the white pebbles that covered one of the plots, placing the plaque, a small multi-coloured wooden horse that Charlie had carved and a tiny replica Viking ship safely in the depression and covering them with the stones. On top he placed an urn in which he had planted some lily of the valley (Lilekonvalj). These tiny white bell-shaped flowers on a thin stem had a wonderful fragrance, something that Charlie had always cultivated in their garden and that had been for him a childhood memory, a carpet of forest floor that bloomed in May in the forests of his Swedish homeland.

Chapter 32

August 1939

It was mid-afternoon on a Friday when there was a loud rapping on the front door. Lizzie was still in full mourning as Charlie had only been gone for four weeks. She had all the curtains closed thus the house was almost in darkness. Margaret and Harry were both at work so she decided to ignore this unwanted intrusion to her sorrow. However, the intruder had not left; a male voice called out and she thought she recognised it. In her severe black clothing and netted hat she made her way to the front door, trying to look though the stained glass panel that allowed in the light and gave a degree of vision. She could make out three figures, all dressed in black.

It is said that people have four main emotions, joy, sorrow, anger and fear, all other emotions being made up of a combination of these. The opening of the door led Lizzie to experience a rush of several of these. Standing almost in a line were three men in Royal Australian Navy uniforms, in the middle her precious son Carl. The initial joy of seeing him made her burst into tears though the sorrow of him being somewhere at sea and missing his father's funeral was still smouldering. Lizzie ushered them inside; she had now been snapped out of her depression as a mother's duty called.

Carl explained that their ship had returned to port for a few weeks and the crew had been given leave. The navy was assembling a convoy of troop ships and their ship would be one of the naval escorts. He had invited two of his shipmates, both of whom came from interstate, to stay with his family.

Lizzie eyed the two with suspicion. Carl was now thirty-five, shorter and heavier than she remembered. The uniformed male to his left, the tallest of the three, looked about the same age. He had a round, gentle face, was balding and in some way his stance reminded her of Charlie. The other was much younger. He had a smug look and he made her remember a line that her son Francis had used from a play he had studied at school. The quote was from the Shakespeare play *Julius Caesar* that she thought went something like, "let me have men around me who are fat, sleek headed men that sleep at night, he has a lean and hungry look, he thinks too much, such men are dangerous".

Margaret and Harry were both delighted to see their much older brother and to meet his friends. They were also pleased to see their mother, a rejuvenated woman, once again fussing over the prodigal son. Over dinner of thick Irish stew, homemade bread and bottles of beer that the men had brought with them, the two friends were introduced. Steve was in his thirties and came from

Williamstown in Melbourne. He was married and had a daughter. All these facts met with Lizzie's approval. She explained that her parents had arrived in Melbourne when they had emigrated from Ireland and that she had been born in Little Lonsdale Street in the heart of the city. Steve said that he knew the narrow street and had often walked up it, commenting on its steepness, with his family after they had caught the ferry from Williamstown, across the harbour and up the Yarra River to the dock near Flinders Station. They had been on the way to visit the botanical gardens, a favourite of his wife.

It was then Ronald's turn. He indicated he was called Ron and was originally from Gladstone in Queensland but his parents had divorced, his father now living in Rockhampton and his mother and brother on Magnetic Island. He mentioned he was twenty-two,

'The same age as me,' Margaret added, a degree of delight in her voice.

Two strikes in Lizzie's mind, divorce and the fact that Margaret was showing some interest in this assertive young man. Twice he had interrupted her and he had also talked over her, a character trait that Lizzie was not used to.

Despite her internal concerns Lizzie, for one of the few times in her life, held her tongue, but only because Ron was Carl's guest. Plans were made for the next day. Margaret had to work in the morning but as Ron had not previously been to Sydney, Saturday afternoon would entail a trip to Bondi Beach. Harry and his girlfriend

Christine would go and as Keith was due home from boarding school for the weekend they would also take him. Carl and Steve declined the outing as they had already planned a day at the horse races at the Randwick track.

Margaret went directly from work on a tram that operated from Circular Quay, along Oxford Street, heading for the North Bondi tram terminus. She had asked her two best friends, Monica and Constance, to come with her. The girls were to meet the others at the Bondi Surf Pavilion. This large two-storey construction had been completed in 1928, replacing the old Bondi Castle bathing sheds. The new building was a mixture of Georgian revival and Mediterranean style, the beach facing colonnade thought exotic. It had changing areas, Turkish baths, shops, lockers, a gym and upstairs ballroom. Margaret carried in her bag a one piece costume called a swing-skirt because it was wider at the bottom. By the end of the 1930s men had moved from wearing two piece swimwear, the "twosome" where a top zipped, snapped or buttoned onto the inside of the shorts, to only wearing briefs, high waisted, knitted rayon, satin look Lastex trunks with a cotton belt. The trunks also had a small coin pocket on the side that buttoned closed. Harry had lent Ron a pair of his that featured a Hawaiian print that had cost Harry one pound and thirty-nine pence. Harry had also lent Ron a pair of his white with black trim rubber beach sandals.

The girls all giggled when they were introduced to Ron. He had stood waiting near the entrance to the change area, posed shirtless, emphasising his darkly tanned, muscular body. He had selected a place on the beach at which Harry, Christine and Keith were already lying on beach towels, their bodies in the direct sun but heads shaded by a large red, white and blue striped sun umbrella. Harry reluctantly accepted that Ron was a bit older and seemed to want to pay for everything but found him controlling and a bit demanding. He didn't ask, just told.

Christine was a true beauty and had supplemented her income from working in a local dress shop with modelling for the Jantzen swim company. Her photograph had appeared modelling swimsuits and sunglasses in *McCalls*, a large format magazine. Her pictures showed necklines that plunged at the back, sleeves disappeared and sides were cut away and tightened. With the development of new clothing material, particularly latex and nylon, swimsuits gradually began hugging the body, with shoulder straps that could be lowered for tanning. Modesty in design also gave way to the health and fitness movement. Women were encouraged to participate in exercise, though only in ways that were deemed ladylike. At the end of the 1930s tanned skin was no longer considered a sign of the working class and became fashionable. Boyish silhouettes were a thing of the past and women sought a shapelier shape.

The day was pleasant enough but on the way home Christine mentioned that she found Ron a bit sleazy. She couldn't explain to Harry exactly why, he just made her feel uncomfortable. When Carl told Harry that he thought they would be spending the evening at a club in Kings

Cross, and would he like to join them, Harry declined; he didn't smoke or drink and he and Christine had already planned on going to the movies to see the Mickey Rooney film, *Love Finds Andy Hardy*.

Margaret, however, was excited at the prospect and again asked her two friends to join them. The three girls had all dated local boys but none had been allowed to go to The Cross, a place with a very bad reputation. Carl chose not to tell Lizzie, he just said he was taking Margaret to meet some friends in town and not to wait up for them, she would be safe with three big, strong, sailors to protect her. At the time Kings Cross was considered the most modern part of the city. There were gaudy new neon advertising signs and a liberal attitude to an increasingly bohemian lifestyle. This had resulted in a growing number of nightclubs and jazz bars offering meals, entertainment and increasingly, alcohol. Breaches of the Licensing Act by venues were regularly featured in the daily papers.

The boys had chosen the 50-50 Club also known as the King's Bridge Club in the Chard's Building in William Street, Darlinghurst. The club was run by Phil "the Jew" Jeffs and had the reputation as Sydney's best illegal casino and sly-grog nightclub. Jeffs was a well-known identity in the city's nightlife. He had gone into temporary hiding during the intense Consorting Squad campaign of the early 1930s and had severed his ties to the cocaine-prostitution racket. Carl had heard from fellow seamen that the club was a safe place to be as Jeffs had developed "an understandings with the police". From 1937 it was widely believed that Jeffs' club was immune to police investigation thus clients were not going to get caught up in a police raid.

The three girls spent most of the night talking to Steve as unlike Carl and Ron, he knew he had a family to support and wasn't willing to gamble. Where Carl lost, Ron won both at cards and dice. Eventually it was Steve who chaperoned the girls home, Carl and Ron not wanting to leave. It had been fun, at least for a little while. The excitement of being somewhere that they knew they should not be, the thrill of watching Carl and Ron gamble, the atmosphere, though filled with thick choking tobacco fumes, had glitz and colour. Though the girls had worn their best floral prints on chiffon cocktail dresses, they were amazed at the beautifully dressed women in the club with their cape dresses, the flutter sleeves and fitted satin gowns. Hollywood trends would now appear to be the driving force. Of their group, Ron especially seemed to look and acted as if he belonged.

The 1930s had seen the athletic body of boxers, swimmers and Superman become the ideal male figure. His clothing reflected this new shape with its emphasis on broad shoulders, thin waist and tapered wide legs. It was Monica who had commented on the similarity of appearance between Ron and her favourite actor, Clark Gable. She had seen most of his movies from his first leading role in *Dance, Fools, Dance* in 1931, then the romantic drama *Red Dust* in 1932, where his interaction with co-star the reigning sex symbol Jean Harlow had made him MGM's biggest male star. Monica had been thrilled when he won the Best Actor award at the Academy Awards in Frank Capa's romantic comedy *It Happened One Night*. The last of his films she had seen was where he played Fletcher Christian in the 1935 *Mutiny on the Bounty*. It was this swashbuckling naval character, a young dashing lieutenant, challenging authority that she saw in Ron. Sadly what Monica and most of his fans did not see was that Clark Gable, like many leading actors in Hollywood, was a chain smoker and a high functioning alcoholic who struggled with commitment. Another trait that Ron would prove to share with the leading man.

Margaret was flattered that her friends were impressed with this young man who appeared to be showing interest in her; yes, deep down she was a romantic. She guessed most girls her age were, holding idealised views of reality. She did have a strong attraction towards Ron, and there was a connection. His focus had been on her at the beach; he had even held her hand as they jumped in the cold waves breaking around them. He had danced with her at the nightclub, even complemented her on her dancing, and most important he had commented how pretty she looked in her dress. She rationalised that perhaps all young men drank too much when they were out with other males and she was sure he would have stopped gambling, but he was winning.

The following day a tall sailing ship, the *Padua*, which had been in Sydney Harbour as part of an around the world tour was leaving at midday. This was a four-masted barque with a height of one hundred and sixty-eight feet (51.3 metres) and a crew of over two hundred and fifty, the ship having been built in Germany in 1926. The ship was propelled by both sail and two, eight cylinder diesel engines. Ron had told them that he would like to see it, with Keith adding that he would like to get as close as possible so as to see the ship under sail. Plans were made to take a ferry from Circular Quay to Manly then a bus to the old Quarantine Station and a walk out to North Head. Harry decided he would also go, as he didn't want to miss out on the spectacle.

'For old time's sake, some fond memories of our father.'

The plan was to finish the day with a late afternoon swim in the netted shark-proof ocean pool at Manly then travel home. Margaret also asked her cousin Kathleen to come as though she had originally been very close with Margaret's older sister Irene, and was nine years older than Margaret, they had become good friends and she valued Kathleen's opinion.

Good plans don't always work and this one fell apart when Margaret twisted her ankle part way along the rocky cliff top at North Head. Disappointedly, Harry pronounced that they would have to head back.

'Can we still go? Please, please,' Keith asked excitedly.

'We'll be careful, I promise. Kathleen will stay with me.'

With a note of sadness and deepening disappointment in his own voice, Harry answered that it would be too dangerous for them to go on alone.

Ron spoke up. 'I could help Margaret back, it's only sprained, if we take it very slowly we should get back about the same time as the three of you. If a bus comes and you're not back we can head home so someone can look at her foot. Is that all right?'

Ron's suggestion was eagerly accepted and the three headed towards the harbour entrance as Ron helped the limping Margaret, putting his arm around her waist to take the weight. After about ten minutes of slow progress, he said, 'Here let me help you.'

He picked her up in his arms and started to carry her.

'No, I'm too heavy.'

She wriggled and as she did they both tumbled off the path into the long grass. They rolled and laughed and when they came to a stop at the bottom of the grassy slope Ron lent over and kissed her. She pulled away and winced in pain.

'Is your ankle still hurting?'

'Of course it is. What a stupid question.'

He stood up and reached down to pull her up. This was the first time they had been alone as up to now the boys or one of Margaret's friends had been around, basically acting as chaperones.

'There is a flat rock over there. I'll carry you to it and we can take off your shoe and have a look. I've done some first aid training and if it is a strain giving it a light massage will help.'

He gently massaged her ankle and then ran his two thumbs up and down the muscles in her calf.

'Is it sore here?'

'No.'

'Good, I like touching you, I reckon you fancy me.'

Margret pushed him away, confronted by his forwardness. The short bus ride was in deathly silence. Neither of them spoke about what had happened.

After an hour or so in the water and baking in the late afternoon sun, Harry arrived with Keith and Kathleen. The rest of the afternoon was filled with chatter about sailing ships and Ron's sea adventures.

Upon reaching home Lizzie fussed about, wrapped Margaret's ankle and confined her to bed. Lizzie wouldn't allow Margaret out of bed the next day but she darted in and out, "to keep up her spirits". Ron was noticeable by his absence. In the late afternoon he returned from wherever carrying a large bunch of flowers. After only one week with the Carlssons Ron asked Lizzie if he could marry Margaret. Lizzie immediately refused,

'You have only been here a week, how can you get to really know a person in that time. Plus you will be gone in a few days, off at sea for who knows how long.'

Ron knew this was the truth; he was also aware that the reason the ship's crew had been granted leave was the belief that war was imminent in Europe and Australia would become involved. On the 3rd of September 1939 it was announced that Australia was at war.

Margaret was taken aback when her mother told her that Ron had proposed. He hadn't mentioned it to her, they had hardly spoken in the last four days. Margaret didn't know what to say. She liked Ron, he seemed to get on very well with Harry and Keith, he was good looking and the navy was a type of job. She liked the idea of being married, and was flattered that a person like him would ask her. Kathleen and her friends had all liked him, she even thought them a little jealous.

Eventually Lizzie relented, saying that if they waited until he returned during his next leave and they both still felt the same way she would approve. To Margaret's surprise Ron seemed to accept that answer, leaving her.

Ron left for his next voyage two days later but was back in less than four months, his ship again preparing to support a convoy. Though times were harder as the country lurched into war, Ron still carried on his versions of courting, taking Margaret out each day but her mother would not allow them out during the evening. Ron spent some of his time with Harry and his mother helping in their charity work and attended mass with the family. This commitment to the Church stood well in Lizzie's eyes. He had not lied about his religion; Lizzie had presumed he was a Catholic; he didn't feel the need to tell her that he and all his family were atheists.

'A belief and commitment to God is a good sign in a man.'

Although once they were married Ron's only visit to a church was for funerals.

Lizzie had kept up her work within her local church but was not sure how she felt about a career Vatican official becoming the new pope. Eugenio Cardinal Pacelli had been the secretary of state to Pope Pius XI and had taken the name Pius XII. She liked the fact that he was not too old, only sixty-three, and in his second month as pope had asked the leaders of Italy, France, Britain and Poland to attend peace talks in the Vatican; at least it showed the Church was making an effort. The previous pope, who they all called the Pope of Peace, had also worked to heal the rift between Church and state and in December 1938 had attacked Italian anti-Semitism. However, as priests were being persecuted in Italy and Germany, Pius XI in his March 1937 encyclical spoke out against the evils of Nazism.

On a sadder note the prime minister, Joe Lyons, who Charlie had always liked as a leader, had died. Charlie had not been happy that during the Great Depression, Lyons had abandoned the Labor Party to join the conservative side of politics as the leader of the United Australia Party. But Lyons' cautious economic approach had won him public support as unlike many countries he had been able to deliver on his promise of economic stability. Known as Honest Joe, his personal popularity had been a major factor in the government's re-election in 1934 and 1937, Joe becoming the first prime minister to win three federal elections. Replacing him had been Sir Earle Page, the

Country Party leader, a person Charlie had disliked because he had caused the dismissal of one of his favourite leaders, Billy Hughes. Billy had been the president of the Coal Lumpers' Union in 1905, third leader of the Australian Labor Party in 1915, leader of the Nationalist Party and seventh prime minster of Australia from 1915 to 1923, thus the ideal leader in Charlie's mind. When the Country Party gained the balance of power in the 1922 election, Page had demanded Hughes' resignation as a price to form a coalition. Lizzie was unhappy with Page's replacement Robert Menzies, a liberal, United Australia Party leader who had visited Germany in 1938 and strongly supported the policy of appeasement, making political, material or territorial concessions to an aggressive power in order to avoid conflict. She had read Neville Chamberlain, prime minister of England's quote of the year: "There has come back from Germany to Downing Street peace with honour. I believe it is peace in our times." Like many she was in disbelief.

Lizzie had also disapproved of Menzies, called Pig Iron Bob, having been in dispute with the union movement in November 1938 when they held a ten week strike in an attempt to stop the export of pig iron that was bound for the Japan Steel Works in Kobe, Japan, to produce military materials.

On a personal note, Lizzie felt the loss of one of her own heroes, William Butler Yeats. His early poetry had recounted Irish folklore and legends and used vivid natural imagery. He had believed that literature could shape a country's identity and as such contributed to radical Irish nationalism. Lizzie had trouble understanding the meaning and imagery of Yeats's poems but always treasured his two books, *Fairy and Folk Tales of the Irish Peasantry* published in 1888 and *Irish Fairy Tales* published 1892. While willing to admit that her literary skills were not as good as many, she enjoyed drawing, specifically the imaginary characters of Irish myth. She drew pictures for Maria and Irene of the mercurial trooping faeries filled with mischief and good deeds and sudden unpredictable changes of mood or mind.

Unlike the "Fairy" from a Latin word *fatum* meaning fate, young, playful, cute and pure of spirit, "Faerie" from Gaelic were usually considered evil and mischievous. Lizzie would draw the solitary but industrious Leprechaun as a mischievous little bearded man, wearing a coat and a three-cornered hat, and his dissipated cousin the Clurichaun known for his great love of drinking and a tendency to haunt pubs, overindulging in sensual pleasures then riding home on backs of sheep.

There were drawings of the eerie wailing Banshee who warned of death, a sad creature, the spirit thought to be of women who died in childbirth, such as Bean-Nighe or washerwoman, washing the bloodstained garments of those about to die. There was the fearsome Phooka, a goblin who lived among ruins. These creatures from Celtic folklore were shape-changers that could take on various terrifying or pleasing forms, the most common forms being an eagle, bull or a sleek black horse with flowing mane and luminescent golden eyes. In folklore the only person to ride a Phooka was Brian Boru, High King of Ireland who ended the domination of Vikings in Ireland, ruling from 1002 to 1014. The Phooka was famed for giving humans a wild ride unlike the Scottish Kelpie that she had drawn for Anders' wife Jane, which takes its riders to the nearest stream to drown and devour them. In Ireland the Kelpie was called the Each-Uisge or Aughisky and the slightest smell of sea water sent them wild.

Ireland did have its own water spirits, whose sole delight was to drown children. Lizzie had told her children of them in an attempt to keep them safe, away from the waters' edge. To encourage them to be careful where they walked Lizzie also told them of the Pixy-Led and Stray-Sod faerie that if trodden on would cause you to become lost or at least be unsure of your way. They had laughed when she explained the only way to break the spell was turning your coat inside out and wearing it that way.

Perhaps the characters she enjoyed drawing the most were the mermaids and merrows. Though her mermaids were always beautiful with long flowing hair, she would still draw them half human and the lower half fish with blue-green scales. The male merrows were extremely ugly with claws and webbing between their fingers on stubby fin-like arms. They had red noses because of their love of brandy, and pig-like eyes. Yeats had claimed that these creatures could transform into "little hornless cows" that grazed in the pastures of the meadows. Charlie had told her he had seen such creatures while sailing off the west coast of Africa. He called them sea-cows, large plant eating mammals in some estuaries and shallower coastal waters.

Chapter 33

The final straw

Following the death of Charlie, Lizzie was left with only two children at home. Her youngest, Harry, was eighteen and working as a cabinet maker when his father died. Though he was never close to his mother he had a sense of responsibility to care for her. Margaret was twenty-two but soon to be married and was preoccupied with planning to relocate to Queensland.

Britain had declared war on Germany on the 3rd of September 1939, and in November of that year the Australian prime minister, Robert Menzies, announced that the existing reserve force, the Citizen Military Force, or militia, would be bolstered by conscription. One of the first pieces of legislation passed by the new Commonwealth government after Federation had been the Defence Act of 1903, which provided for the raising of an Australian Army. The act established the government's right to conscript men for self-defence in the event of war. Thus on the 20th of October 1939 the Universal Service Scheme was introduced.

At nineteen, Harry received the notification of his conscription into the army, but applied for a delay to allow him to support his recently widowed mother, Lizzie. He was granted twelve months but in May 1941 left, taking up arms for his country. Harry was actually a bit of a prude and was easily shocked about matters related to sex and nudity. Though he loved Christine she was only nineteen when he had to leave for the army. He promised that he would write but never did. He worried he would be killed and leave her alone, thus neglect resulted in loss. She found someone else.

Harry joined the 35th Battalion, Australian Infantry Force and sailed for Europe on the troop ship *Manoora*. While the convoy was at sea, concerns were raised about a Japanese invasion force, thus the ships were redirected to Western Australia. He wrote to his sister, bemused by the fact that he with two other soldiers guarded a long section of the Western Australian coast. He wondered, with their three rifles, how successful they would be at holding back a Japanese invasion force, a country with over a hundred million people with a strong army and navy. Fortunately he was never faced with this dilemma, spending nearly half a year sitting in his tent watching the waves and swirling seagulls.

After the May 1942 Battle of the Coral Sea, a major naval battle between the Imperial Japanese Navy and naval and air forces of the United States and Australia, the Japanese decided to invade New Guinea. Harry's battalion was then reassigned to New Guinea to bolster the troops already on the ground. While still in the jungles of Papua, Harry was called into the command post and informed his mother had died. There was no opportunity for his return to Sydney thus he headed back to his fellow troops. At times of war, guilt and self-interest often have to be put aside. He rationalised and tried to put his feeling in perspective. His mother had lived a full life and they had not been close for years, yet around him young men, his comrades with whom he had developed close bonds, were being killed each day.

Lizzie had found herself alone. Both her sons had left to fight; Carl was in the navy overseas and Harry was in the army in New Guinea. Her daughter Margaret had settled on Magnetic Island with Ron's family. Lizzie had recently received a letter from her explaining that Ron had been injured in a naval engagement and while recuperating needed her help on the farm. The letter also informed Lizzie that she had another grandchild, a girl born a few weeks earlier.

Lizzie pondered on the fact that perhaps none of them would return. There were families in the street who had received telegrams indicating a loved one was missing or dead. Lizzie waited each day for hers; fate had not been kind and she expected them.

At first it was depression. She had a persistent feeling of sadness; she struggled to sleep and had lost her appetite. Her energy levels were also low and whereas she had always been the first up preparing the family for the day and the last to bed, finishing off the chores, now her reason to structure her day, or even get up, was gone. There had been moments when the thought of suicide had crossed her mind but there was God. He would not forgive people who did that; deep down she had lost her religion but not the fear associated with her faith.

Her friends had started to comment on the forgetfulness, at first in a joking, jovial way but later with a tone of concern. She knew herself that she was frequently confused especially in the late afternoon and during the nights, so started writing lists of what she had done and who she had seen. She was also annoyed at her inability to recognise common things. Lizzie had always been stern and slightly superior but she was becoming more irritable and lacked restraint.

Mrs Martin, a previous foe who now rented a house across the road, called in daily. She started to do a bit of cleaning and Lizzie's shopping, but this further isolated Lizzie. The local priest also visited but Lizzie was not welcoming. She had lost so much and slipped into a type of paranoia, believing that the priest was only interested in her worldly possessions. He had talked about bequeaths, about donating to charity, but whereas in the past this would have been considered and where possible supported, that was then, when she had a husband and large family to support and encourage her.

Fearing that she was losing control, and with her children far away facing constant danger, Lizzie was convinced by Mrs Martin that she needed to give someone a power of attorney, someone like her who was willing to help her each day. This Lizzie did. Sadly, in 1942 Mrs Martin convinced a local doctor that Lizzie was a danger to herself and she was admitted to the Gladesville Mental Hospital. Due to overcrowding Lizzie was transferred to the Bloomfield Psychiatric Hospital in rural Orange. Because of the war, many of the male staff had joined the armed forces thus staff were stretched in trying to care for the over thousand patients housed in twenty-three ward buildings. The spacious grounds provided many with a serene environment in which to recover but Lizzie found herself restrained based on previous reports of self-harm. The paperwork that came with her showed the reports had been made by a Mrs Martin, Lizzie's carer.

When Lizzie died in August 1944 her body was moved back to Sydney in a lead-lined coffin to be interned with her family in the Rookwood Cemetery. Sadly she was alone. Her daughter Margaret had been sent a telegram but was unable to travel, her husband refusing to consider the trip with their baby.

When Margaret finally managed to get back to Sydney it was June 1945. She arrived at her family home to have the door opened by a woman she did not recognise. Mrs Martin explained that she had purchased the home and its furniture and had disposed of all personal possessions on the assumption the family had deserted Lizzie and did not want them. Though Margaret had received the telegram about Lizzie's death, Mrs Martin stated that she had the legal right to do this and lied about not knowing how to contact any family members. Margaret noted this stranger was wearing her mother's pearls and a cameo that she and Harry had purchased for their mother as a birthday present.

'Please wait here while I get something from inside.'

She closed the door, leaving Margaret standing outside. Returning she handed Margaret an envelope which turned out to contain a cheque that was made out for a fraction of the worth of her parents' home. The other item was an old case that contained a few of the family's old photograph albums and the family's Swedish Bible. Mrs Martin again closed the door and though Margaret knocked and called out, her distress was ignored. As she turned to leave, her parents' car drove down the side lane, a young man driving and Mrs Martin in the passenger seat.

It was now Margaret who felt alone. She knew she should do something, consult a lawyer, seek help, but all she could do was cry and make her way back to Central Station for the long train trip back to Queensland. How could she tell Harry? No, she wouldn't, not yet; he faced enough conflict fighting in a war. It could wait till he was home, face to face; yes, that would be best.

Epilogue: 1946

As a warrant officer based at Wewak, New Guinea, Harry being a single man remained after the declaration of peace in September 1945 supervising a prisoner of war camp for Japanese prisoners until their repatriation back to Japan.

In April 1946 he was surprised and delighted to be met by his sister at Sydney's Central railway station. She stood holding his niece but he could tell from the expression on her face something was wrong.

That afternoon Harry and Margaret stood holding hands, alone but sharing their misery. It had been nearly four years since their last face to face meeting and written correspondence had been limited and guarded. Though sharing is considered a basic component of human interaction, ensuring a person's well-being, what they now shared just increased frustration and annoyance. In her letters Margaret had avoided telling Harry the whole truth, but now he was home she had no choice. The two metre white marble cross threw a shadow, a pointer to their past, their heritage, their memories and now the focus of their anger.

Over time they had learnt to accept their priest's "will of God", that in life we all face challenges and suffering, but the way it ended, how could they forgive or forget. Unspoken, both thought about revenge.